Caught by the Blizzard

Adele Huxley

ISBN-13: 978-1503322516
ISBN-10: 1503322513

DEDICATION

To every English teacher I ever had. Thank you for teaching me, pushing me, making me diagram sentence after sentence.
I had to learn the rules before I could start breaking them and boy, is it getting fun now!

CONTENTS

	Prologue	8
1	Chapter One	16
2	Chapter Two	30
3	Chapter Three	42
4	Chapter Four	48
5	Chapter Five	62
6	Chapter Six	102
7	Chapter Seven	129
8	Chapter Eight	164
9	Chapter Nine	185
10	Chapter Ten	213
11	Chapter Eleven	242
12	Chapter Twelve	278
13	Chapter Thirteen	289

PROLOGUE

Liz

My eyes returned to the bag of blue liquid dangling over my head. I watched it drip, drip, drip. I followed the snaking blue tube all the way down to the crease of my elbow before it disappeared behind a criss-cross of medical tape. The nurse had said it would take a little while to kick in but I was already starting to feel woozy. The way my skin buzzed wasn't entirely unpleasant and I thought I might actually enjoy a high like this given any other circumstance.

I laid in my hospital bed fully prepped for surgery and absolutely terrified. Just as the panic clenched my chest with overwhelming strength, my father appeared, pulling a chair close to the edge of my bed. I knew what he was going to say before he even opened his mouth.

"You don't have to do this." He brushed my bangs away from my face. The concern in his eyes was enough to break my heart. Lord knows the last thing I wanted to do was cause this man any more grief in his life.

I closed my eyes and smiled tightly. “I do, Dad. I don’t have any other choice.”

His head dropped and he nodded. “I had to say it one last time.” He looked up and reached for the stuffed horse I had beside me. “I’m glad you have Dapples.”

The drugs lowered my defenses. The walls I normally had securely in place seemed little more than chicken wire. As he held the stuffed animal in his big hands, hot tears rolled down my face. “They said I could bring him in. It’ll be like when I got my tonsils out. That’s when Mom got him for me.” My voice quivered. I was stoned, scared, and on the verge of sobbing.

“Oh darlin’…” he said as he hugged me. I rested my chin on his big shoulder, blinking back the tears as best I could. My eyes found the IV bag and I was surprised to see it mostly empty. I hugged him with my right arm, the only thing that wasn’t connected to some monitor or needle.

“It’s okay, Dad. She always said Dapples would make sure everything went smoothly.” I took a big, shuddering breath as I tried to calm myself. My voice sounded so young, so tiny. “It’ll be like she’s here.”

My father hastily wiped tears from his face as he returned to his seat. I saw how bloodshot his eyes were and I knew he hadn't been getting enough sleep. I hated that I was the reason for it. "I'll be here when you wake up."

"I know. I love you, Daddy," I replied. I could hear the slur in my voice, my tongue unable to shape the words properly.

That's one of the last moments I remember clearly. At some point the nurse came in to say the doctors were ready. I hugged my dad one last time and they wheeled my bed out of the quiet room and down the hall. The ceiling lights became a blinding kaleidescope. A mask was put over my face and a woman with a kind voice asked me to count backwards from one hundred.

My next memory was waking up in the recovery room, disoriented, and in the worst pain of my life.

Bryan

I closed my eyes and visualized the course for the billionth time. *Steep drop, immediate right turn. Tuck into the corner and push through to the straight away. Hold tight through the launch and land ready for the hard left bank.* My muscles twitched and tightened as I waited in the gate, imagining the course opening before me. The official clapped me on the shoulder and gestured for me to move forward.

"You got this, man. Blizzard!" Dave said with a nod. It always amazed me how much shit he'd give me during practice but come race day, he was nothing but support. What more could you ask for in a teammate?

I gingerly pushed forward into the gate using my poles. I pulled my goggles off the top of my helmet and let my eyes adjust to the pink hue. The specialized lenses were designed to reduce glare and improve depth perception, something I'd desperately need as I flung myself down the mountain at 72 miles per hour.

The small crowd at the top of mountain grew quiet. I tried not to think of my mom and Angela waiting at the bottom, my dad somewhere along the course with binoculars. I took long, deep breaths and tried to steady my heart. Adrenaline coursed through my system. As always, I struggled to keep in check, keep it from overpowering me. *I rule gravity. Gravity does not rule me.* I repeated it like a mantra.

Beep. Beep. Beep. BEEEEEP.

Like a trained thoroughbred, I leapt from the gate at the sound of the bell. It was a good start. I got a good push right out of the gate, my edges digging into the snow as I propelled myself forward. Within seconds, I was barreling down the the hill. I tucked into the right turn, poles snug against my body. The rush of wind filled my ears even through the helmet. My sight felt heightened, hyper-aware. I maintained a stiff squat through the straight and braced myself as the ground fell away from under me. I flung my arms out for balance, knowing the difference between first and fourth place could be determined by one awkward landing.

Good! Fuck yes, I thought as I touched down. I cornered left and felt the lines were better than any of my previous runs. I remember I smiled at that thought, something I never do in the middle of a race.

The next big turn on the course was shadowed, a large outcropping of rocks obscuring the sun. I knew instantly I'd taken the turn a little too aggressively, practically jumping onto my edges at full speed. I felt the skis judder beneath me and my world blurred. I was down before I even had time to cry out.

I remember taking a hard impact on my left hip before my head smacked against the ground with sickening force, enough to knock me out for a few moments. When I finally came to, I was on my back, wrapped awkwardly in the orange safety fence. I could hear voices in the distance calling my name but I didn't answer. All I could think about was how blue the sky was, such a beautiful, deep azure.

A face hovered above me. "Hey man, you with me? Oh thank fuck, he's awake. Hey man, where's it hurt?"

I tried to shake my head. I wanted to ask him to move so I could look at the sky just a little longer. He repeated his question so I finally said, "It doesn't hurt. I'm alright."

A quick intake of breath hissed through his teeth and he left my field of vision. As I listened to him speak into a walkie-talkie and I vaguely wondered at the panic in his voice. “We need ski patrol up here now and get the ambulance prepped.”

At some point, I blacked out completely. My next memory was waking up in the recovery room, disoriented, and in the worst pain of my life.

Líz

"This is the house?" I asked as the Kayla pulled the Jeep into the drive. "No way. You're fucking with me, right?"

Kayla grinned at me with just a touch of smugness. "Told you it was nice." Okay, maybe more than a touch. She flipped her dark hair over her shoulder with a gloved hand and smiled like she'd designed the place.

"Um, nice? That thing is bigger than my dad's house," I said nodding towards the three car garage. Aren't you gonna park?"

"I've gotta head back to the mountain in an hour. Besides, Noah gets funny when we park the Jeep in there next to his cars." She rolled her eyes as we climbed out. "Anyone in the house can use the Jeep, just so you know." The frigid air whipped right through my sweatshirt but I was too shocked by the cabin to care.

Nice wasn't the word for it. Palatial. Enormous.

Impressive. The cabin was nestled into the side of the steep mountain, a winding staircase leading up to the front door. The whole place seemed to be made of windows. Icicles glittered from the peaks of the snowy roof. As I stood, mouth hanging open, a young woman in a bikini top came out on the deck and waved down at us. Her long brown hair hung down the railing as she leaned over.

"Hi! Do you need help with the luggage?"

"No, we're good thanks," Kayla responded. "Be right up."

I kept waiting for the punchline. This seriously couldn't be the place we were staying in all season. It was only when Kayla hefted one of my bags out of the trunk and started carrying it up the stairs it began to sink in. Kayla might take jokes too far sometimes, but she'd never resort to physical labor unless she had to. I quickly ascended the stairs behind her, shaking my head in disbelief.

As I walked through the wide doorway, I was hit with a blast of heat. With no winter clothes to speak of, I was thankful for the warmth. Even in the walk up from the car, it felt like the cold had already seeped into my bones. I dropped my suitcase and gaped at the interior, repeating my comment. "You're fucking with me. I was expecting some little shack in the woods. Not this."

The house was essentially one big, open room. The entryway opened into the huge kitchen which then flowed into the plush living room. From where I was standing, the place looked as long as a football field. Recessed lights glowed from between the wood beams, although with all the bright windows, they didn't need to be on. Everything looked brand new and specifically positioned, like it'd been staged for a showroom.

"What, you didn't believe me?" she said over her shoulder. Kayla was already wheeling my stuff down the hall to the left while I stood in awe.

"You could've sent me a couple photos or something," I mumbled as I followed. I ran my fingers along the stone accent wall in amazement.

Her laugh echoed down the hall. "But then it wouldn't have been such a good surprise. Here, this is your room. It's the biggest but it's also the coldest 'cause it's on the corner."

It could've been a freezer for all I cared. It was beautiful. The king size bed faced a large fireplace with a stone mantle. I walked towards the bank of sliding doors that opened directly onto the deck. My view was a thick forest of snow covered pine trees, like something out of a real estate catalog.

"Open the door to your left," Kayla said with a grin. She pulled her long, dark hair back into a ponytail.

The door swung open and revealed my en suite bathroom. There was a huge vanity, two sinks, and a rainfall shower, but that's not what I noticed first. "It's all windows!" I exclaimed. "How am I supposed to shower in here?"

"The windows steam up pretty quickly and it's not like there's anyone out there waiting for a show. Like that'd bother you, anyway."

I sighed. "You know I don't do that stuff anymore."

"You like?"

"Kay, I *love!* I'm utterly speechless. To go from Ashville to this…"

Kayla sat on the edge of the bed and patted the mattress beside her. "Which is what I wanted to talk to you about."

I groaned, turning to take in the amazing space that was mine, all mine. "Can we not right now, please? I just got here." I knew this conversation was coming but I'd hoped she'd at least let me unpack first. I chewed the inside of my cheek but made no move to sit beside her.

"Babe, come on, it's *me.*"

We'd met freshman year. We'd been placed on the same floor in the dorm and both had roommates from hell. It'd been an instant friendship and after tearfully begging the RA, we managed to switch and move in together. We'd been inseparable ever since. She was the only person in the world who knew what my life was really like, mostly because she'd pulled me into the lifestyle.

I shrugged and tried to sound blasé. "I'm just taking a little time to myself, figure out what I'm really doing with myself."

Kayla frowned. "Okay…now try the non-bullshit version you didn't tell your dad. Don't get me wrong. I'm super glad you came out here, but what about school? The semester isn't even over yet. I didn't expect you until after Christmas. Did you skip finals to come out here?" I glanced at her and had to look away, the concern on her face threatening to make me cry.

I scoffed. I crossed my arms and started pacing around the room. I couldn't lie to Kayla as easily as I could to everyone else. We shared the same skills and with them came the ability to see right through any lies or manipulations.

"You know I had nothing but gut courses. I turned in my papers weeks ago." Even I didn't believe it. The truth was, I'd stopped going to class a couple weeks after the semester started. I was definitely going to fail anyway, so how could a couple final exams help? Not to mention, I'd played the dead grandmother card three times already. Someone was bound to figure that out eventually. Truth was, I had to get out of North Carolina and fast.

"What did your dad say when you told him?" Kayla knew I was a daddy's girl at heart. Hell, the reason I'd gotten into so much trouble was because I wanted to make things right between us.

"I just told him I was burning out at UNC, which isn't a complete lie. Told him I wanted to gain a little life experience and then start next fall with a clear head." My heart ached at the idea of my dad all alone in that small house on base. It felt so far away.

"And see? That's not a lie either. I promise, you'll get some wicked life experiences here." Kayla got up and squeezed me tightly around the waist, picking me up a couple inches off the floor. She might've been a few inches shorter but she had crazy, hidden strength. "I've missed my Lizzy!"

I begged her to put me down which she did only when I started laughing. In Colorado for less than an hour and I was feeling better than I had in months. *I totally made the right decision,* I thought as I hugged her back. “Alright, show me the rest of this place before you go. Who was the girl?”

“That was Morgan and Spencer is another roommate, but I think he’s out on the slopes right now,” she said as she led me back to the hallway.

I arched an eyebrow and chuckled. “On the slopes, eh? Already using the lingo?”

“I have to look and act the part, don’t I? Anyway, it’s not that much different than surfing. I was exactly what they were looking for,” she said with a twirl.

“A first generation Korean girl from California that comes to the Rockies via North Carolina. Makes total sense. How did you get picked from so many potential candidates?”

“They’re progressive,” she laughed.

She gave me a quick tour of the rest of the house, finishing up on the huge wraparound deck. There was a built-in stone grill and a six person hot tub. I still couldn’t believe this was the place I was staying for the winter. I felt like I was in some kind of dream.

As we stood at the railing of the deck, I heard a strange sound off to my right and turned to look just in time to see someone whizzing past on their skis. I looked at Kayla quizzically.

"Door to lift. All these cabins share an exclusive slope so you don't have to drive to the resort. Just slap on your board and head down. Pretty cool, huh?"

"Great use to someone who can't ski."

"You'll learn quickly. And if you look way down there," she said pointing down the slope towards a small grove of pine trees, "you can see the pond where we all go ice skating. Well," she laughed, "more drinking than skating to be honest."

The biting cold finally won over admiring the beauty, so we headed inside to the kitchen. Kayla grabbed a couple bottles of water out of the huge stainless steel fridge and handed one to me. "What are you doing for money then?" she asked looking sideways. "You have some saved from the club, right? Miss stripper who doesn't take her clothes off," she giggled.

I took a sip of the water and shrugged. "I'll be alright." She knew I'd made good money dancing but didn't exactly know my account balance. *$289,420, but who's counting?* I thought. The amount made me happy, the way I'd gone about earning it didn't. Dancing at a nightclub netted about a tenth of the total. The rest came directly from the…arrangement…I'd made with Rick. Kayla didn't seem impressed by my silence. She crossed her arms and pouted a little. I knew that expression all too well and it spelled trouble.

I groaned. "Come on, spill it. I knew this was all too good to be true. What is it? Are there cameras everywhere or something? Am I online right now?" I waved around the kitchen to the imaginary cameras.

"Nothing like that. You know the guy Noah I mentioned earlier? He's the last roommate but…his dad also owns the house." She said it quickly, like ripping off a band-aid.

"Rich kid complex?"

"Like you wouldn't fucking believe. That's not the best part. Not only does his dad own the house, he owns the entire mountain. His family just bought the resort a couple months ago."

"Alright, I see where you're going with this," I said. The picture was starting to clear up but there were still a few hazy spots.

Kayla grinned, pulling her ponytail over her shoulder with a tug. "I *could* get you a job at the mountain maybe or…" I raised my eyebrows in question. "Or you could start selling again with us."

I should've known better. I shook my head, twisting the cap back on my bottle of water and setting it down silently. Leaning forward on the counter, I looked at her, disappointment evident on my face. "You're dealing again?"

"It's not like Ashville, I swear. We've got the market cornered here, tourists coming in an out all the time. The town has three cops, Lizzy. *Three*."

I loved her and would do just about anything for her, but why did I think Kayla would ever change? A hundred things I wanted to say fought through my brain, struggling to get to the surface. None of them were very nice, so I had to temper my reaction a bit.

"Kay, you got out of town just in time. You weren't there to see how everything went down. I can't go back to that again, I can't." I bit my lower lip to stop it from quivering with anger. I'd lived it but it was still difficult to talk about. She'd closed herself off, ran away, left me to fend for myself.

She held her hands up defensively, eyes wide. "Okay,

fair enough, I thought I'd offer. You seemed happy with the arrangement you had with Rick—"

"Rick's in prison and I barely managed to avoid getting caught myself," I snapped. As close as we were, I still resented the way she'd left me so suddenly. I knew she did it to protect herself, but it felt an awful lot like abandonment. "I still had to check in with my parole officer when I wanted to come out here."

"Alright…it's just that the last time we talked, you said Rick—"

I spun on my heel. "Can we just *not* talk about Rick, please? He's out of my life, for good. The whole point of coming here was to figure out what went wrong and how I can get back on track." I pushed the hair out of my eyes and drew a ragged breath. Everything was still so raw. I hadn't developed the coping skills necessary to deal with it. I leaned my hands on the counter, unable to meet her eye.

"You never went to visit him, did you?" It wasn't a question. It was a realization. "Jesus, Liz. Have you at least talked to him on the phone?"

I shook my head. "Just once, right after he went in."

"God, he's gotta be so pissed," she muttered to herself. I often call her 'my sister from another mister' but when it came to Rick, we couldn't be more different. I was just about to respond when she spoke up. "Ah shit, I have to go." I turned and leaned against the counter, anger bubbling under the surface. I knew we'd have to talk about everything at some point, but for her to bring him up ten minutes after I arrived…

"Listen hon, I'm sorry. You just take the winter and chill. We're gonna have a ton of fun, I promise." She took my hands and smiled at me, white teeth shining. "Starting with tonight, yeah? We're gonna go out when I get home from work. You and me." She hugged me tightly, her scary-strong arms squeezing the anger from me. Within seconds, I was laughing again.

"Alright! Let go you freak, I need to breathe!" I pulled away and forced myself to smile through the swirl of emotions. "Sounds perfect."

After Kayla left, I returned to my room and started unpacking. It was only going to be a short trip, so I hadn't brought much more than the essentials. I still needed to go shopping for a jacket and other warm clothes. The winters in Jacksonville, North Carolina never got cold enough to warrant a full winter wardrobe.

I set my suitcases on the huge bed and unzipped them, letting the lids fall open. My breath caught in my throat, eyes instantly blurring with tears. A framed Polaroid photo my dad normally kept on his dresser at home was centered right in the middle of my clothes. *Dad must've snuck it in there before I left.* In the photo, my mother was about my age, flying down a snowy slope. She wore a matching white hat and glove set, a bright red scarf flying in the wind behind her. She was grinning wildly, my smile so similar to hers. As I held it, my fingers brushed a note stuck to the back. I flipped it over and read my dad's handwriting out loud.

"Just like her, I'm sure you'll be a natural. Have fun, be safe. Love, Dad."

Falling to the bed with a sigh, I held the photo in my lap, tears running freely down my cheeks. It'd been eight years since she'd died and I missed her like crazy every day. And every day, I wondered what my life would be like if she wasn't gone.

Bryan

I made great time and pulled into Tellure Hollow by early afternoon. I'd gotten there the old fashioned way; road maps and my memory. Since it'd been well over fifteen years since I'd been there, the folded road maps in the passenger seat of my truck had done most the work. I pulled into a parking spot right on Main Street and cut the engine. I took a slow breath as I stepped down, a shot of pain rocketing through my left side as my knee straightened. I leaned against the frame of the truck and I waited for the throbbing to become manageable.

The town looked pretty much the same as I remembered it. Small, quiet, and at the foot of the snow covered Powder Mountain Ski Resort. Most of the local businesses were on this main street. In fact, I'd passed the closest Wal-Mart and McDonald's about an hour earlier. I smiled to myself as I shut the door. *This is exactly what I need.*

Working the kinks out of my joints as I moved, I

slowly walked up the street. The town had received half a foot of powder the night before making everything look picturesque. Glittering snow coated every roof and streetlight, dusting the Christmas decorations that were strung across the street. Thankfully, the sidewalks had all been cleared. I was still wearing the sneakers I'd left California in and I really didn't feel like slipping on any ice.

The streets were busy. The thriving tourism the resort brought in kept the town alive. I was hoping the transient town would help me keep a low profile for the season, just long enough for me to sort my shit out. Hard for people to learn much about you when they were only in town for a couple days. And if they did, it didn't matter. They'd be on their way soon enough.

About half way up the street, I walked passed a ski shop called Freddy's. I stared at the orange wanted sign in the window and felt compelled to go in. With my background, I could grab any job I wanted at the mountain but something about the cluttered store front called out to me. A bell above the door chimed as I walked in. It took a moment for my eyes to adjust to the gloomy store.

The shop was dimly lit, mostly because it was stacked floor to ceiling with every bit of ski and snowboard gear that'd ever been made. Boards hung from the ceiling, coats and pants pinned to the walls…the place was a mess and I loved it instantly. The unmistakable smell of hot wax hit me like a slap across the face.

"Hello?" I called out.

"Hey! Back here," a voice called out from the back of the store. I picked my way through the tight aisle toward the tuning shop in the back. I spotted an older man hunched over the work bench, smoothing the melted wax into a snowboard with a small iron. He looked at me above his glasses. "Can I help you find something?"

"A job, if you're still hiring." My voice sounded scratchy. It'd been days since I'd spoken to anyone.

"Oh yeah? You got experience?" He gave me The Squint. I knew he recognized me but couldn't put his finger on exactly where. I could almost see the wheels in his brain turning. As famous as I was in certain circles, I got The Squint several times a day. You'd think I'd eventually get used to it but each time was like a spike of irritation, a reminder I could never leave my history behind.

"Enough to know you're gonna burn that wax unless you keep moving," I said nodding to the board. That seemed to refocus him and he jumped back to the board with a curse.

I glanced around the workshop and was surprised that it was fully decked out. Stone grinder, edger, everything. I spotted a full rack of equipment obviously waiting to be tuned. He finished up and set the iron down, giving the wax time to cool.

He wiped his hands on a red handkerchief and shoved it in the back pocket of his jeans. “Position is part time, minimum wage, under the table, and weekends are mandatory.”

“Sounds perfect.”

He squinted at me, the wrinkles around his eyes deepening. “You ain’t a townie, so how long you stayin’? Too many transients around here nowadays.”

“Well, sort of. I haven’t been here in a while, but my grandfather was born and raised on Cedar Street. I’ll be here for the season then after that…” I trailed off. I didn’t know how to continue the rest of that sentence.

“What’s your name, son?”

“Marsh, Bryan Marsh.”

The Squint turned into The Look, which I almost hated more. The Look said, “I know you! You’re that guy who…” Sure enough, the old man’s eyes got wide as he finally placed me.

"You're The Blizzard. Bryan The Blizzard. Aw shit son, I saw that crash live on TV, such a shame what—"

I waved my hand, trying to get the guy to just drop it. I knew what happened. I was there for fuck's sake. "Yeah, well, I go by my real name now."

He leaned back on the workbench and crossed his arms. "I knew your grandfather, you know. Good man. I think he's buried in the cemetery, ain't he?" I nodded. "Ah, well then, guess that does make you a sort of townie." He sniffed and fell silent, still staring at me. "Well, just cause you was good at usin' skis don't mean you're good at fixing 'em. Come here and show me what you can do."

I stepped around the workbench, doing my best to conceal my limp. It wasn't usually that bad but the long drive had stiffened everything up. If the old guy noticed, he didn't show any indication of it. I ran my hand over the snowboard, feeling the thickness of the wax. The board was obviously well used but only a few years old. Grabbing the rectangle of Plexiglas, I held it in both hands and found the sweet angle against the board. As I pushed it, long curls and flakes of wax dropped to the floor.

The smell hit me again. What is it about scents that draw out your emotions like they're on strings? Pictures, scenes, bittersweet emotions. My entire life had revolved around the things in this shop until abruptly, it didn't.

A memory of my dad showing me how to hot wax my skis popped into my mind. I couldn't have been older than ten. He'd caught me trying to do it on my own, ruining Mom's expensive iron in the process. Rather than yelling at me, he just sat me down and showed me the correct way to do it. That was Dad. Always instructing, always teaching. He even went out and replaced the iron so I wouldn't get in trouble.

Blinking back tears, I finished buffing the board down. I bent close and blew the remaining flakes away, finally stepping back so the old man could take a look. After a brief inspection, he gave a curt nod, once again looking me over.

"Alright then, can you start Saturday?" he asked thrusting his gnarled hand towards me.

I nearly winced as I shook it, the strength of his grip surprising me. "Absolutely…"

"Walter, people call me Walt."

There was something I instantly liked about him, something sage and earthy. I looked around the shop and smiled. *Screw anti-depressants and PTSD groups. This might be the sort of therapy I need.* I again noticed the big rack of equipment waiting to be tuned and nodded towards it.

"I can start sooner if you want, help you with all that."

Walt scoffed and started loosening the vice. "Folks don't mind waiting for quality work around here. I don't do quick turnaround like the bastards up there," he spat in the direction of the resort. "All these are locals. Not to say, I wouldn't mind taking some that out-of-state money from time to time." He picked up the board and set it in the rack opposite, taking the tag and stapling it to an invoice. "But if someone comes in here demanding it back in an hour, they can fuck right off. That's what that Roberts fella is offering up at the mountain and if you ask me, they probably don't do a damn thing for the money." He looked like he'd just tasted something bitter.

"Alright, good to know," I nodded. I'd spent enough time in various ski towns to know the locals rarely got along with the tourists. His anger wasn't anything new to me. "Listen Walt, I appreciate it. I've gotta go get settled but I'll see you Saturday, alright?"

He'd obviously gotten himself all worked up. He grunted and waved a hand at me, still muttering under his breath about the resort. I chuckled to myself and made my way out of the shop. I took note of a bar across the street called the Gritty Cask. *Probably a tourist trap,* I thought, *but could be a good place to get something to eat later.*

As I made my way back down the street, I saw a bright green Hummer parked through three of the diagonal parking spots. One of the town cops circled the truck taking down the information, obviously as unimpressed by the gleaming chrome as I was. He noticed me looking as I walked past and rolled his eyes, returning to his ticket pad. I was doing a quick sweep of my truck to make sure the guy hadn't scraped it when the driver approached.

"Oh come on, I was just in the store for a minute. Don't you have anything better to do?"

"Sir, your vehicle is blocking—"

"Yeah, alright." The driver had a hawkish face, his blond hair peeking out of his perfectly placed knit hat. I stood in stunned silence as he pulled out his wallet. "How much is it?"

The cop looked at the money in the guy's hand and then back to his ticket pad. "It's not like that. You'll have to go down to the station to pay it in person or you can send in a check."

The blond huffed. "My money spends just as well now as it will later. Here, take a hundred and we'll call it even, alright?"

Shaking my head, I climbed into my truck and left the cop to deal with it. This town had definitely changed since the last time I'd been back. The layout of Tellure Hollow was pretty much the same since it was first settled back in the 1800's, but with a new influx of people, the town limits had grown over time. I parked on the street in front of the house, taking note that I'd have to find a local kid to come shovel the drive for me. Still mid-afternoon, the sun had already disappeared behind the mountains, bathing the neighborhood in an odd glow.

I grabbed my bags out of the truck and looked at the resort looming over the entire town. The stark white trails stood out against the dark forest of the mountain. I noticed the hill to the side was sprinkled with huge faux log cabins, expensive places that were occupied only a fraction of the year. "That's new." With a sigh, I fumbled with my keys and trudged through the snow to the one bed, single floor palace I'd call home for the next couple months.

With no cable, no internet, and no time like the present, I set about unpacking my meager belongings. When my mom had heard I was planning on coming out for the winter, she'd originally wanted me to stay at the hunting cabin. I wasn't ready to face that place, so she did the second best thing and found this rental. She also went to the trouble of hiring someone to come through and tidy up, stock the fridge and cupboards with some staples I'd need. I thought she was being ridiculous, but as tired as I was, the gesture was very welcome. All I had to do was put away my clothes, but even that proved difficult. A few minutes later, I found myself frozen in place, an open photo album in my lap. I sat back in the piles of clothes and flipped through it.

My therapist had helped me put the album together, each photo agonizingly chosen to evoke a memory or emotion. He'd designed exercises around the album but I could barely look at each photo for more than a moment. It brought the past to the present with such startling speed. If I wanted to get better, I knew I had to face it, even if it was only for a moment or two a day.

It started slowly, baby photos of me and my brother. Those I didn't mind. As the pages turned, I grew. Me and my dad on the slopes when I was little, him guiding me with a belt and straps around my waist. Suddenly, I was a teenager. A photo of my mom and brother at the finish line cheering, ringing loud cowbells. Even at that age there were signs for The Blizzard.

My throat felt like it was squeezing shut. I gritted my teeth and turned the page, knowing what photo was next. Angela and I in our prom outfits, smiling, young, happy. Then it was my dad standing beside me on the podium, biting my gold metal between his teeth, arm slung over my shoulders. He looked so proud…

Hot tears flooded my eyes but I tried to push through. The next photo was a profile shot of Angela and Mom at the line, waiting for me to finish a race I'd never complete. The following pages were filled not with photos, but newspaper clippings. I slipped my finger under the page, hand trembling as I willed myself to look. Instead, I slammed the album shut with a curse and jumped to my feet.

"I need a walk," I explained to the empty house. "I'm too tired for this right now."

Liz

Tellure Hollow was one of the cutest, smallest towns I'd ever been in. The snow and mountains made the whole area look like a postcard. After borrowing one of Kayla's jackets and a pair of boots, I decided to grab my camera and walk into town. The excitement of being in a new place, such a different place, made me antsy. I wanted to throw myself into the experience head first.

I must've taken a hundred photos as I walked down the hill. Everything grabbed my attention. The way the light glinted off the snow, making it look like a sea of diamonds. The way the tree branches hung heavy…the bright blue sky. The cold was invigorating and fresh, triggering my already overactive imagination.

Daydreaming comes naturally to me. Usually, an idea or an image will trigger an avalanche of *and then's* and *what if's*. Before long, my new life in Tellure Hollow unveiled itself before me. I'd own a small but lucrative photography studio, not portraits but artistic. The wealthy tourists would all fight over my work. With all the time I spent on the mountain, it was inevitable that I'd become a world-class skier. I'd probably start a program that organized free lessons to underprivileged kids, win some award, meet the President.

By the time I reached the bottom of the hill, I was wrapped up in my own little dream world. I approached a bridge I hadn't noticed when Kayla was driving up to the house. Thankful that I'd thought to buy fingerless gloves before I left, I lifted my camera to my eye and started snapping photos of the river. I crouched down and took a few shots between the ornate concrete design of the railing.

One of things I love most about photography is how it favors the brave. To get some of the most incredible shots, you have to be willing to get down and dirty. You can't be afraid to climb or hang or risk bodily harm for a good photo.

I noticed the shadows from the bridge looked really cool on the rippling water below. There was a ridge of ice overhanging the edge of the rushing water that that caught my eye. I hooked my leg through one of the holes to secure myself, brushed away a patch of snow with my arm, and leaned over. Just as I was framing the shot, two big hands grabbed me around the waist and yanked me back.

"Hey!" I shouted, spinning to see who'd grabbed me. I

was suddenly face to face with a pair of smoldering hazel eyes that reminded me of a stormy ocean. I blinked a few times, refocusing on the guy's face and holy shit, was he hot. His lean, chiseled face was hidden under a couple day's worth of stubble. Shaggy brown hair stuck out of his black knit hat and that jaw…that jaw could've cut glass. His expression was confused, nearly angry, as if I'd put him out in some way. A list of obscenities caught in my throat, a strange choking sound coming out instead.

"Hey yourself. I just saved you from hypothermia. Don't you know how dangerous that is?" His voice was deep, slow.

We stood looking at each other for a moment before I realized his hands were still on my waist. A part of me wanted to step into his arms while another wanted to tear off my glove and slap him. Regaining a bit of my sense, I glared and pushed them away. "Like I give a shit. I was fine."

He licked his lower lip quickly and stepped back, half smiling at me. That smile could've bought him a ticket straight to Hollywood. "And they wonder why chivalry is dead."

Regardless of how hot he was, I didn't appreciate being touched, an issue I hadn't quite gotten over since dancing at Rick's club. "You didn't open a door for me. You nearly shoved me off a bridge," I snapped.

"That's not the way I see it. I saved you from a near certain death." The way he said it so matter-of-factly drove me crazy. I huffed through my nose, feeling like a bull about to charge.

"Whatever," I said, turning to walk away. God, how infuriating! I'd just gotten into the zone and that shot was going to be amazing. After a few steps down the sidewalk, I spun back around, unable to drop an argument that easily. "You could've destroyed my camera."

"But I didn't. The least you can do is buy me a drink to say thanks." The half smile turned into a full grin. What the hell is up with this guy? I had to give it to him, his delivery was smooth, straight-forward without coming off as obnoxious. Still, I wasn't about to let another pretty face sweet talk their way into my life. Not again. I tightened the scarf around my neck as he strolled closer. I wanted to turn and walk but couldn't seem to pull my feet up.

"Then at least let me buy you a drink to apologize for saving you." His eyes were so intense I could barely stand to meet them. I felt unbalanced, like the world had begun to rotate around us. He reached out and touched my arm. I reacted without thinking, slapping his hand away with enough force to startle both of us.

“Don’t touch me!” I snapped. I hated the shocked look on his face, like I was some kind of lunatic. I held my hands up defensively. “Listen, thank you, fuck you, whatever. Pick whichever one you find relevant and leave me alone.” Was this what I’d become? I didn’t know what else to say to him so I walked away…like I always do. I reached the other side of the bridge before the urge to look back became too much.

I glanced over my shoulder and saw him leaning against the railing, arms crossed, smirking as he watched me walk away. It made me want to slap and kiss him all the more. Instead, I just flipped him the bird and somehow, it felt better doing it with my fingerless gloves.

Bryan

I was trying to look cool as she walked away but internally I was already kicking myself. *Seriously? That's the way you're talking to people now? That's the way you treat a gorgeous girl like that?* But it hadn't been a total disaster. She *had* looked back and I was pretty sure I'd spotted a small smile on her face, hidden behind her hair. Alright, she'd flipped me off, but I liked a little attitude.

I didn't want to be a creep and watch her walk away, so I turned and headed in the opposite direction for a couple minutes before winding my way back home. It felt good to stretch my legs even though the cold aggravated the pins holding me together. Once back at the house and with my muscles nice and warm, I settled on the floor and started my physical therapy exercises. My therapists and doctors had done everything they could. Now, it was a matter of sticking to a strict regimen and listening to my body.

That was the hardest part. I'd lived my entire life on

the edge, pushing my body to the absolute limit. My dad always told me that real growth came when the pain kicked in. “If it’s hurtin’, it’s workin’,” he’d always say. I had to completely retrain the way I approached obstacles in my life. My PT was not only a physical battle to recover my body, but a mental one as well. The therapists hadn’t helped much in that area. My instincts told me that Walt and his shop might be the best therapy for me.

As I went through the routine, I found my mind drifting back to the girl on the bridge. I’d spotted her as I rounded the corner. Stunning. Gorgeous. The kind of girl guys fight over and fight to keep. She seemed so wrapped up in taking those pictures, I didn’t feel like she’d catch me watching. It was like she was seeing snow for the first time. At one point, she’d picked up a handful of it and threw it in the air, just to watch it scatter in the breeze.

When she leaned over that edge, I was sure she was going to slip and fall in. I’d run to her before I’d even realized it, my feet carrying me across the road and leaving my self-imposed hermit life behind. When she spun around and I looked into those amazing ice blue eyes, I’d felt that pull. God, I hadn’t felt that sort of pull towards a woman in forever. Years. I wanted to kiss the red flush on her cheeks, taste her lips…

I sat up with a grunt, wiping the sweat from my face. I didn't come to Tellure Hollow to scramble my brain any further, no matter how pretty she was. I got to my feet like an old man with arthritis and walked to the bathroom. As the shower heated up, I looked myself over in the mirror. This was the one thing the shrinks had been able to help me with. After months of therapy, I was finally able to look at myself without wanting to scream or tear my world apart.

My eyes traced the diagonal scar that ran from my left shoulder down towards my chest. I didn't allow myself to look any further down to my hips and legs, but I knew what was there. As the mirror began to fog and I stepped into the shower, I wondered how that girl would react if she saw my scars. I hadn't been with anyone since the accident…

"Christ dude, she cursed you out and walked away without saying goodbye," I muttered. *True, but she did look back,* said a voice in my head.

The Gritty Cask was a lot better than I'd hoped. With a small brewery in the back and a bar menu with real food, it was a welcome slice of civilization. I'd always found ski towns were hit or miss when it came to good food and drink. After an hour in the bar, I felt right at home.

The crowd seemed to be a good mix of locals and tourists, all blissfully coexisting with the help of a little liquid lubricant. I'd stuffed my stomach with the first hot meal I'd eaten in days and found myself playing pool with Dale. He was at least ten years older and a hundred pounds heavier, the kind of guy I'd want behind me in a fight.

"So you make snow up at Powder Mountain?" I asked as he took his shot. He missed the seven and sunk the cue ball with a curse.

"Don't you mean Angel Vista?" he said with disgust.

I frowned, wiping the blue chalk on my jeans. "I didn't know there was another resort around here."

"There ain't. They went and changed the name, if you can believe it. Who does that? Who changes the name of a goddamn mountain?" He took a big gulp of his black stout and slammed it back down on the table, froth spilling over the edge.

"I don't know, man. Did someone buy it?" I bent down, my hip screaming in pain. I nicked the side of the one ball and knocked the nine into the corner pocket. "It's kind of rare when a mountain isn't privately owned."

Dale's eyes glimmered with an anger enhanced by three pints of Guinness. "That mountain belongs to us. Our families settled here and that dickhead Richards comes in here, flashing his money around, and *buys* our goddamn mountain?" Small droplets of spittle fell on his ginger beard as he spoke, his voice growing louder with each word.

An equally large guy in a Polaris hat appeared from the crowd and clapped Dale on the shoulder. "Hey man, take it easy. The guy's kid is over there." He tilted his head to the far corner of the bar where a mix of guys and girls were playing quarters. "From what I hear, the kid's just as bad."

The guy he pointed to was the blond asshole from the street earlier and wouldn't you know it, he had his arm slung around the gorgeous girl from the bridge. Figures. Just my luck. I turned away and took a sip of beer. *Better off. I have to concentrate on getting healthy,* I thought. Still, I was disappointed she was already here with someone.

"Ever since that guy bought the mountain, things changin' around here. All these out-a-towners, no offense, they bring in drugs, get into trouble. Used to be a nice quiet place you could raise a family but anymore," Dale grew quiet but a vein still prominently throbbed on his neck. He glanced at the pool table and chucked his stick down. "Fuck this. I need a smoke. Hey, good meeting ya Bryan. I just need to cool off," he said as he nearly crushed my hand in his strong fist.

"No worries," I replied. Even after one day in town, I'd gotten a good lay of the land. It hadn't even occurred to me to research the mountain before I packed my stuff and drove up. Powder Mountain had always been a local gem. The resort and town didn't have the glitz and amenities as other resorts. Anyone who found their way to the town did so because they were serious about skiing, not spa days and Michelin star restaurants.

I grabbed a seat at the bar and ordered a water. My doctor had prescribed a new pain med a couple weeks before I'd left and I hadn't tried drinking while on it yet. Already, my one beer felt like three. Shockingly, my stomach rumbled. Just as I was about to reach for the menu to order a second dinner, a delicate arm appeared from behind me and set a full shot glass down.

"Thank you for saving me."

My heart skipped when I heard her voice but I also cringed. Our first meeting had been a disaster. Still, I smiled to myself but didn't turn, my eyes focused on her reflection in the mirror in front of me. "So you decided that's what happened?" I kept my voice low.

"I think *you* thought you were saving me, which I didn't need by the way, but I figure it's the thought that counts. Here. Peace." She nudged the shot glass closer to me.

"And what if I was just looking to grope you a little? I'm walking along, see a pretty girl bent over, figure what the hell? Worst thing she can do is slap me." I said it with a shrug, hoping she was the kind of girl who could take a joke. Please, *please*, be the kind of girl who can take a joke because that came out a lot gruffer than I'd intended.

"That's cute."

I finally turned in my barstool, meeting her gaze directly. Her blue eyes had softened since I'd last looked into them but there was still a bit of an edge. I had to fight every instinct to keep my gaze from traveling down to her chest. The gray sweater she wore hugged her curves like it was painted on.

"What's cute, exactly?"

"That you think a slap is the worst thing I could do to you." Her nostrils flared a little. I could already tell she was that awesome combination of cute and sexy, smart and mouthy. Damnit. I really was in trouble with this one. Nothing turned me on more than a girl who could banter.

“Let’s start over. I’m Bryan.” I held my hand out. She glanced at it and her smile broadened. That smile warmed places inside me that’d been cold for far too long.

She slipped her soft hand in mine. “Liz. Well, Elizabeth,” she corrected as she sat beside me. “Beth, Lizzy, Eliza. Everyone seems to pick their favorite.”

“Multiple personalities?” I ask arching my eyebrow.

Liz glanced at me out of the corner of her eye before knocking back her shot. “Something like that.”

I traced the lip of the shot with my finger as I debated whether or not to drink it. I was already feeling fuzzy but I didn’t want to ruin the peace offering and risk running her off again. After promising myself I’d drink extra water to compensate, I downed it. I tried my best to take it like a man but I involuntarily shuddered as the liquid burned down my throat. I coughed into my fist and looked at her accusatorily.

“What the fuck was that?” I said between coughs.

“Fireball,” she giggled.

I coughed again and squinted at her with watering eyes. “I think *that* was the worst thing you could’ve done to me.” I took a big gulp of water to cool the burning.

“Not quite. You pick the next round then,” she said giving my arm a playful slap.

My heart stopped for a moment. *She wants to stay for another round!* Her forwardness was perfect. I'd been so long out of the game I wouldn't have ever been able to approach her. All I had to do was not fuck it up.

A girl shouted in celebration from across the room. She was in the group with the owner's son, jumping up and down like she'd just won the World Series. Liz turned to look over her far shoulder and I took the opportunity to really take her in. Her brown hair was pulled back in a high pony tail, just brushing the tops of her shoulders as she turned her head. Even sitting, I could tell her proportions were knockout. Just looking at her thin waist and round hips drove me out of my mind. If this girl wasn't a model, she was seriously wasting her God-given assets. Before I could get too worked up, I looked away and cleared my throat, drawing her attention.

"So Liz, what's the most dangerous place you've ever taken a photo?" My voice sounded like I hadn't used it in years and for the life of me, I couldn't swallow my nerves.

She tilted her head at me, surprised by the question. She looked up, deep in thought. "Hmmm, that's a good question. I've shot rodeos before, but that's not too scary. I've done drag races." She counted each one on a finger until her eyes went wide. Jumping up in her seat like she'd sat on a tack, she exclaimed, "Oh, I know!" She grabbed my knee as she continued. "I was on the edge of a big dune at the beach during a hurricane. I was on my stomach leaning over the edge and it was sketchy, like, *really* sketchy. I wanted to get a shot of the foam shooting up into the air but I wasn't thinking. The ridge on the dune had been formed because the waves were eroding it all away. I remember feeling the sand shift underneath my elbows and I barely managed to roll away before it collapsed under me."

Between the intensity of her eyes and being touched by a woman for the first time in years, it was difficult to concentrate. "Wow, okay. You have some type of death wish with water?"

She shook her head and removed her hand, the absence leaving my knee cold. "Nope, but I got the shot," she said with a wink. "I'll show you sometime. Speaking of shots, it's your round."

"Anything but that last shit," I laughed.

"Alright, whiskey?" she offered waving the bartender over. Out of everything, she had to pick that. Whiskey to my temper was like spinach to Popeye. I'd already complained enough about the drinks, I didn't want to look like a wuss. I vowed to drink three glasses of water.

“Sounds good.”

Thankfully, the alcohol loosened my nerves because they weren’t going to unwind on their own. Like everything in my life, my flirting and conversational skills were a bit rusty but things started to flow well. The longer I talked to Liz, the more I felt like myself. She was clever, sarcastic but not mean. She was quick to laugh and I loved trying to make her smile.

As we were getting to know each other, I found myself dodging direct questions about my past. I didn’t want to go into it, didn’t know how. She hadn’t given me The Squint and didn’t seem to know my history, so I wanted to keep it like that. It felt too good to be *me,* not Bryan The Tragedy. I didn’t want to lie to her, but I hadn’t quite worked out how to tactfully answer some questions yet.

A half hour later, my head was really starting to swim. It was with a twinge of concern that I realized how drunk I’d gotten, but I was too far gone. All the water in the world wouldn’t have saved me. Liz wasn’t exactly sober herself, nor did she seem to care or notice.

“So what do you do?” Finally, a question I didn’t have to avoid.

“I work at Freddy’s, just across the street actually.”

"And what do you and Freddy do?" She took another sip of her drink. My eyes dropped to her pink lips, wondering what she'd do if I just pulled her stool over and kissed her.

I blinked my fantasy away. "No, it's Walt. I'm not sure who Freddy is. Maybe Walt's name is really Freddy. Maybe he's like you, with all the multiple personalities." She laughed at that, so I continued. "Who are you when you're Elizabeth."

Without missing a beat, she replied, "Daddy's girl. He's the only one who calls me that anymore."

"Lizzy?"

She hooked a thumb over her shoulder, pointing to the pretty Asian girl hanging off the douche bag. "Her best friend."

"Liz?"

She shrugged but gave me a half smile. "Trying to figure that one out still."

I nodded, knowing exactly what she was talking about. "What about Beth? What's she like?"

Her expression clouded, the humor falling from her face. I winced, sensing that I'd poked a sore spot without knowing. "She doesn't come out very much anymore."

Before I had a chance to salvage the conversation, the blond asshole with a pinched face appeared between us. He was wearing a thick sweater that probably cost more than I'd earn in a week at Freddy's. Liz tensed as he wrapped his arm around her.

"There you are. I've been looking for you," he said completely ignoring my presence.

"Here I am," she replied, shrugging his arm free from her shoulders. Her discomfort was obvious.

I'd spent a lot of time working on keeping my temper in check, but in my drunken state, I decided to speak up. "Don't worry. I've been taking real good care of her." He turned his hawkish face a fraction towards me, but kept his eyes on Liz.

"Kayla was looking for you. Why don't you come back with me?" His hand slid down her back and under her arm, fingers lightly grazing the side of her breast. That's when the therapy went out the window and my whiskey temper decided to step in.

I rose to my wobbly legs and grabbed him by the shoulder, digging my fingers into his flesh. Part alcohol, part stiffness, I ended up putting a lot of weight into the grip. "I think she can make her own decisions, buddy." That got his attention, his dark eyes rising to mine.

Liz

I swear, my heart had nearly bounced out of my chest when I saw the guy from the bridge sitting at the bar. I didn't think he'd noticed us come in, so I watched him from a distance. Even though I hadn't been able to stop thinking about him the entire afternoon, I hadn't told Kayla about the encounter. What was there to really tell? Some stranger did a nice thing and I'd nearly ripped his head off for it. As we all stood around chatting and playing drinking games, I spent nearly an hour convincing myself that I wanted to make things right because it was the decent thing to do. It absolutely had nothing to do with the fact I wanted to look into those amazing eyes again.

When I'd set that shot down on the bar in front of him, I was fully prepared to make peace and walk away, conscience clear. Maybe get a free drink out of him, but nothing else. I hadn't expected him to be so intriguing and fun. Dear God, one day in town and I'd already found a sexy, smart guy I couldn't stop thinking about. Great. So much for fresh starts. I already loved his dimples and the way his hazel eyes seemed to change color in the light. Even his laugh sounded like a private joke the two of us shared.

I was sober enough to get a good read on him. He seemed genuine but kept sidestepping anything that got too personal. With every touch, brush of my hand, and playful slap, I felt him stiffen a little. At first, I thought he might have a girlfriend or wife but I quickly dismissed it. My best guess was that he was a soldier who'd recently reentered civilian life, hence not wanting to talk about his past too much. I'd seen it enough back in North Carolina. He had the look. Still physically fit, shaggy hair, and a haunted look behind his eyes.

I cringed when Noah had come over. I'd nearly slapped his big nose off his face as he grabbed a little side-boob, but when Bryan put his hand on him, I knew the powder keg had been lit. Why does every hot guy seem to have anger issues? The tension was thick with testosterone and booze, never a good combination. I tried to wedge myself between them but unfortunately the moment for womanly intervention had quickly passed.

Noah looked at Bryan's hand and then to me. Part of

the reason I'd approached Bryan was to escape the handsy creep. From the moment we'd met at the cabin, I could feel him sizing me up. There was a cold and inhuman element in his dark eyes, like he saw everything and everybody as a commodity. He'd made his mind up that he wanted me and didn't hide his desire. Not only was I totally weirded out, but there was something obviously going on between him and Kayla. I wasn't about to get in the middle of that.

"Sounds like this asshole doesn't know who I am," Noah said to me. His smile had all the charm and appeal of a TV evangelist.

I gave him a tight smile, hoping I still had a chance to snuff the fuse. "He probably hasn't had the pleasure yet."

Noah reached across with his opposite hand and plucked Bryan's from his shoulder. He dropped it like it was a sack of shit. Bryan rocked forward and steadied himself on the bar.

"Something tells me it won't be much of a fucking pleasure," he muttered.

They squared off, chins lifted, eyes boring holes in one another. Noah was about the same height and roughly the same build, but didn't bring quite the same confidence. Any muscle Noah had managed to accumulate at the country club gym was purely aesthetic. In contrast, I could tell the muscles hiding under Bryan's long-sleeved shirt served a purpose. After a moment, Noah laughed it off, probably sensing he was outmatched.

"Come on, let's go find Kayla," he repeated. This time, his hand traveled down to cup my ass, trying to guide me home like a lost foal.

"Hey, get your fucking—" was all I managed to get out before Bryan's fist went flying through the air. Despite his obvious drunkenness, he managed to land an impressive punch on Noah's temple. Noah went down, Bryan falling on top of him following the force of the swing. With a growl, he landed a another couple more punches before a few guys in the crowd pulled him off.

I'd like to say I was shocked but growing up in military towns leaves you a little numb to common bar fights. I only react when someone starts flashing weaponry. Bryan rolled onto his back and looked up at me. "Are you okay?"

They say you can tell a lot about what a man's like in bed by how he moves on the dance floor. Well, in my twisted little mind, I believed I could tell a lot about how a man fucks by the way he fights. The passion in Bryan's eyes when he looked at me nearly took my breath away. Passion is passion. Love and anger are pretty close on the spectrum of human emotion. Yes, I realize how screwed up that sounds…

"Alright, the two of you gotta go," the bartender said behind me.

"Wait! He grabbed her, that's all. I was protecting her," Bryan shouted from the floor.

The guy in the plaid shirt holding Noah up looked at me. "Is that true? This guy touched you?"

I didn't know what to say. If I told the truth, I was risking a very awkward living situation back at the cabin. If I lied, I probably would've ruined any chances I had with Bryan which surprisingly, I wasn't willing to do. I looked from one to the other, my mouth hanging open slightly. The guy holding Noah up limply seemed to think I was too scared to respond.

"Alright, that's all I need." He gave Noah a good shove towards the door. I groaned at the pointed look he shot me as he was pushed outside. My inaction had just created an enemy. Great.

Kayla rushed over, slipping her arms through her puffy black coat. She glared at Bryan as he returned to his seat.

"Come on, I'm gonna take Noah back to the house. I don't think he's in any state to be driving." She spat the words in Bryan's direction, his shoulders hunched. She took a few steps towards the door and stopped when it was obvious I wasn't following. "Aren't you coming?"

The last thing I wanted was to get in a confined space with Noah. "No, I think I'll have one more drink here before heading home."

Kayla's eyebrows shot up. "You're kidding me. With this hick? I thought you were done with guys like—you know what? None of my business." She rummaged through her bag and handed me the keys to the Jeep. "If you aren't home in a couple hours, I'm calling the police." She stormed away and out the door before I could respond.

As the bar started to settle and the tension dissipated, I sat down beside him. "Sorry about her," I mumbled. Bryan stared at his bloodied fists as if shocked they were his own. I noticed he was still trembling. He let out a ragged breath and looked at me with those fierce eyes, his temper still simmering. He opened his mouth to speak when two huge hands clapped down on his shoulders. I jumped nearly as high as Bryan did, but I had the advantage of seeing who they were attached to.

Bryan spun around, already gearing up to swing again when the mountain man let go. “Whoa there, killer. I was just coming over to congratulate you!” He held his hands up defensively. Bryan paused for a beat as if catching himself and chuckled.

“Hey Dale.”

I looked between them, the confusion evident on my face. Dale grinned broadly at me, slapping Bryan on the back as he talked. “This guy’s been here for a day and he’s already a hero. Lemme buy you a drink. Goddamn, I wish I’d gotten to smack that little shit. Mind you, his father’s probably gonna sue your ass, but the whole town’ll pay the bill.”

It was a couple minutes before Dale said his goodbyes. I was thankful for the distraction. I’m pretty sure I would’ve dragged him out of that bar and up to my bedroom if he’d looked at me like that one minute more. We sat in silence until a thought popped into my head. My giggle caused him to look up from his half finished beer.

“So is that it? Are you like Superman or something? You go around saving damsels in distress and beating up bad guys.” He laughed loudly, shaking his head.

“That’s exactly it. You’ve cracked the shell, my

identity is exposed." His eyes flashed a little as he spoke, making my stomach flutter. This guy had demons, I was sure of that. But then again, so did I.

The bartender gave him a towel with some ice for his hand and I slid my stool a little closer, picking up where we'd left off before. It didn't take long before he went from pleasantly drunk to completely wasted. If it weren't for the fact he hadn't left my sight for hours, I would've thought he'd taken some drug. I watched him slouch further and further onto the bar with each passing minute. His speech became slurred and it was getting difficult to even hold a conversation with him.

"Are you alright?" I asked him, putting a hand on his arm.

"Can I ask you something?" His eyes were half open but I still found him cute in a goofy kind of way.

"Sure," I said with a seductive hint. My inner flirt wanted to shift the conversation to something a little more risque.

"Can I call you Liz?"

"You can call me whatever you want, as long as you call me," I giggled. I'd always wanted to use that line and it made him laugh.

"Can I ask you something else?" His head was nearly resting on his arms at this point.

I nodded, drawing even closer. "Mmmhmmm?"

"Doesn't your back hurt?"

I furrowed my brow. Okay…not what I was expecting but I could work with it. "No, I do plenty of yoga. I'm really flexible." I bit my lip a little as I gave him my sexiest look but he shook his head. He put his elbow on the bar and rested the side of his head in his hand, squinting at me.

"No, I meant with those," he said nodding to my chest. "They're obviously fake. I was just wondering if you got back pain from it."

Zero to asshole in four seconds. I abruptly pushed away from him. "Are you kidding me?"

"Hey, I didn't say there's anything wrong with them. They're incredible, honest. I just—"

"Why? You think you're gonna get a closer look? What a fucking fucked question to ask someone." I turned completely away from him, already kicking myself for thinking he'd be any different than any other guy.

"Wait, no. I'm sorry, I—" he touched my shoulder and I spun around.

I would've been spitting fire if I hadn't been so

disappointed. I grabbed his hands and slammed them against my breasts, giving him my signature unimpressed look. “See? Now you can go back and tell your buddies you’ve felt a pair of fake tits before. Happy?”

He yanked his hands away and looked at me like *I* was the crazy one. “Yeah, you can go fuck yourself,” I said grabbing my drink. “Where the fuck do you get off talking to me like that?” If there’s anything I was sensitive about, it was my implants. If my temper rested on a hair trigger, he’d just found it.

Bryan sputtered, his surprised and hurt expression the only thing stopping me from giving him a good smack. How could I have been so wrong about him? He’d seemed so…*no, this guy is obviously a complete ass,* I resolved. Shaking with anger, I stormed away, pushing through the crowd to find Morgan and Spencer.

I tried my best to bond with the other two roommates, but I felt like a total third wheel. Morgan was a sweetheart and seemed completely oblivious to Spencer’s obsession with her. One look and I knew he was smitten. Even though he was nice enough, I could tell I was cramping his game. Slowly easing out of the conversation, I decided to finish my drink and head back to the cabin. It’d been a long day. I couldn't wait to turn on the fire and crawl into bed.

My eyes shot to Bryan as he stood to leave. He stopped at the door, glancing in my direction but the glare I gave him ended any ideas he might've had about coming over. If he hadn't mentioned he lived a couple streets over, I would've been concerned about him driving home. At any rate, I figured he'd walked to the bar. Maybe karma would take a swipe at him and he'd fall into a slush puddle.

I drank the rest of my beer, said goodbye to Morgan and Spencer, and walked out to the lot half expecting him to be waiting for me. Was I glad or disappointed when I didn't see him out there? Regardless, as I waited for the Jeep to warm up, I kicked myself for caring either way.

"Great job, Liz. Less than a day and you've managed to get into three arguments with two different guys," I whispered, my breath coming out in a white cloud. "Fresh start my ass."

I pulled out of the lot onto the quiet street. It was a little past midnight and anyone who wasn't at the bar was fast asleep in bed. Not wanting to go home and face yet another fight with Noah yet, I decided to drive around. Tellure Hollow was literally a one stoplight town. I wondered what it was like during the summer. Did the mountain pull in people during the summer months or did it get even quieter?

With the massive mountain looming over the place, it was impossible to get lost. I turned right and left, navigating around the quiet streets until I thought I should probably make my way back to the cabin. As I turned left onto a road that led back to Main Street, I immediately noticed the bright glow of a pickup's red taillights. They looked odd, tilted strangely. My lights streaked across the backend as I turned and I saw the front driver's side tire was stuck in a ditch. I squinted at the scene, slowing as I passed. I didn't see anyone around but judging from the burned out patches of road, the driver had tried to gun it out and failed.

I saw movement in the cab and my heart started racing as I realized the driver might be hurt. It was obviously a fresh accident, maybe they'd hit their head? I pulled alongside at an angle, shining my headlights on the crooked truck. Rushing to the passenger side, I banged on the door.

"Hey! You need help in there?" I heard a groan and a little movement but no response. The engine was still idling, the exhaust filling the light with a smoky haze. I had to really pull at the heavy door to open it. As soon as I spotted the driver, I let out a loud groan. Bryan's drowsy eyes met mine, a bright trickle of red blood flowing from a cut on his head. I nearly shut the door and walked away.

"It's you," he slurred. His smile was the only thing that stopped me from leaving him there to freeze. It was so genuine, like he was actually happy to see me. Still holding the door open, I looked down the street and ran through my options. I could leave him but he might die of hypothermia. I could knock on one of the houses…

"I'm gonna pull your truck out with the Jeep. Turn the wheel towards me." With his head lolling, he tried to pick up a hand but didn't even make it half way. "Turn the wheel towards me." I used my dad's voice, stern, no-nonsense. It seemed to get through the fog of inebriation. Bryan lazily pulled the wheel to the right and I concluded I was correct about the ex-soldier evaluation. "Hold onto it while I tow you out."

I walked back to the Jeep and moved it around to face the truck. I took a little joy in seeing Bryan blink and shield his eyes from the bright lights. "Serves you right," I glowered. I jumped out, detached the winch, and got on my knees cursing him the entire time. I hooked it to the frame and climbed back in the driver's seat. Slowly, I reversed until the line went taut. Keeping the speed steady, the Jeep easily pulled the truck from the ditch.

After putting everything back, I opened the passenger door again. “You can drive home now.”

He scoffed, looking at me with one unfocused eye. “To California? No chance. I’m too wasted…”

“You don’t say.” The neighborhood seemed safe enough and the truck was now parked on the side of the street. He might get a ticket but it’s the least he deserved. His head rolled back onto the seat with a brief snore. “Bryan!”

“Wha…?” he jerked up, blinking repeatedly.

“You’re coming with me. Come on, get out. You can’t sleep here and if you can’t tell me where you live…”

He slid down the bench seat towards me, nearly falling out of the cab. I steadied him against the side of the truck before reaching in and grabbing the keys. I tucked them into his pocket, briefly distracted by how firm his thighs felt under the cold denim. Once secured in the passenger seat of the Jeep, he started to laugh.

“What is it now?” I snapped.

“You’re the Superman now. Super*woman*! *You* saved *me*.” I smiled despite my annoyance. His head rocked forward, chin resting on his chest. Thankfully, he remained quiet for the short trip back to the cabin.

I pulled the Jeep into the heated garage, parking next to Noah's green Hummer and red pickup. I'm not sure how, but I managed to get him upstairs and into the house. Everything was quiet and dark, mostly. There were noises coming from the opposite end of the hall near Noah's room, Kayla probably soothing his wounds. I hadn't quite thought through what might happen if he found Bryan in the house.

I put my arm around his back and guided him towards the living room. He might've been a rude asshole, but he made for a very pliable drunk. He fell backwards into the black leather sofa, sinking in with a groan.

"Stay. I'm gonna see if there's a First Aid kit around here."

After searching all the bathrooms, I finally found the red plastic case under the kitchen sink. I wet a paper towel in the sink to clean up his cut. Flipping through the supplies as I returned to the living room, I didn't notice Bryan had already passed out.

"I don't think you're gonna need stitches but I don't want you bleeding on—oh," I gasped. He'd taken his shirt off and was fast asleep, snoring softly. I couldn't tear my eyes away from the massive scars running down his left shoulder. They weren't fresh but obviously not very old, the scar tissue still red and raw. I let my eyes roam across his lean, athletic body. I bit my lip as I noticed the small patch of hair disappearing into the waist of his jeans. That's how I spotted the other scar.

Checking quickly to make sure he was completely asleep, I crouched beside him. A similar red mark to the one on his shoulder peeked out a few inches above his belt. My fingers reached out to touch it, wanting to trace the red line down until it disappeared beyond the waist of his jeans. He stirred a little before I touched him, causing me to pull back quickly. I wondered what sort of accident he'd been in. Maybe something from the deployment? I glanced at his face and thought, *Who are you*?

There was a strong jaw beneath that unkempt beard. He had crazy long eyelashes and his full bottom lip begged to be sucked. I pressed my own together, resisting the temptation. After wiping the blood away from his forehead, I could see the cut more clearly. It was small and easily covered by a bandage.

"Definitely not the worst injury you've ever had, huh?" I said to his sleeping form. I brushed a curl of brown hair from his forehead and he stirred again.

"Thank you, Superwoman," he mumbled. He rolled

over, facing the back of the sofa. I wanted to lie down beside him, nuzzle into the valley of his spine, and go to sleep. Instead, I grabbed a blanket and tossed it over him, thoroughly confused by my first day in Tellure Hollow.

In my exhausted state, I'd forgotten to draw the curtains over before I'd gone to sleep. The early morning sun reflected off the snow, throwing bright light into my room. Even with the heavy covers pulled over my head, I still couldn't get to sleep. I gave up and laid there, staring out the windows at the serene forest.

I thought about Bryan in the other room. What was I going to say to him? Was I still even angry with him? I held onto grudges like it was a hobby but really, how was he to know my implants were a sore subject. It wasn't that I wanted a boyfriend or even a fling. I just hated that I kept fucking things up with him at every turn. It didn't bode well for any future relationships if I couldn't remain at least civil with someone new.

Throwing my arms above my head, I stretched and let out a long yawn. I quickly threw on some clothes and went to check the living room and sure enough, he was gone. The blanket was nicely folded. There was an indent from his hand on the top where he must've patted it. Tentatively, I put my hand in the spot, spreading my fingers wide to fit. I noticed a note scrawled on a torn piece of paper beside the pillows and blanket.

Didn't want to wake you. Sorry about last night…I can explain if you want…or not.

Thanks for taking care of me.

B

Living in the cabin was actually great. I could feel the tension and stress from the previous few months just slipping away. Everything that'd happened with Rick, the life I'd fallen into when I was in Ashville…it all started to feel like a terrible dream. Everyone in the cabin, including Noah, worked during the day. I spent the days exercising, watching movies, playing around with my photos in Photoshop. With every passing day, I felt like I was closer to finding myself. There'd been a little tension when Noah had come home early one day, but with everyone around he didn't make a scene. It was obvious he wasn't too pleased with me living under the same roof, though. Kayla tried playing peacemaker but the chances of us acting nice were slim.

Kayla hadn't actually gotten around to taking me to lodge until a week after I'd arrived. Early one morning, she came running into my room and jumped on my bed.

"Wake up! You're coming to work with me today," she said bouncing on her knees. "We got over a foot of snow last night, so it's a perfect time to make a video."

As much fun as I was having enjoying time to myself, I was beginning to understand the term "cabin fever." I was ready to get out for a little while, get a change of scenery. I sat up on my elbows, wiping my face with one hand. “Okay, okay. Coffee on the way please?”

“Already brewing.” She skipped off the bed and stopped short at the door. “Dress warm. We’re gonna be outside today and you’re my camera woman.”

I was really starting to feel at home in Colorado. A few days before, Kayla and I had driven over an hour to shop at the smallest mall I’d ever seen. The trip was pretty much all for me. In typical Kayla style, she’d bought all her winter gear from designer stores before she arrived. She looked every inch the snow bunny; furry collared hoods, matching hat and scarf sets. She even had a pair of knee-high winter boots with three inch heels she was currently wearing.

“Are you seriously going out in those?” I giggled as she went clicking out of my room.

“What?” she’d replied, kicking her heel up behind her like a cheerleader. “I figure I can spear the snow like an ice climber.” I had to hand it to her, she rocked the hell out of them. Even though I had the money for all that stuff, I was happy with my more practical choices. With a groan, I rolled out of bed and got dressed.

"It's too high," I said shaking my head. I backed away from the window of the gondola, rocking it as I sat. "It's just way too high."

"It's a mountain," Kayla laughed. "I didn't know you're afraid of heights."

I looked out the side window, the angle of the car roughly the same as the steep hill we were climbing. My ears popped as we rose in elevation. Skiers and snowboarders dotted the trails in the distance, barely more than ants on a hill. "I'm not afraid of heights. This just doesn't feel right." I squeezed my eyes shut and tried to calm my breathing. "Just talk to me about something. Distract me."

"Okay…how did you get your parole officer to agree to you coming out here?"

My eyes popped open. "Anything but that!"

Kayla shrugged. "I'm just curious, that's all. I guess after everything you told them about Rick it's the least they—"

"Seriously, stop. I'll fling myself out of here if you keep talking about it." Not that I'd actually do it, but even the threat made my stomach clench. I gripped the edge of the seat with my gloved hands, my eyes pleading with Kayla.

"Alright." She rolled her eyes. "We should go over what I'm looking for then. Your job is really simple. Make me look gorgeous and keep everything in focus."

"Won't be a problem." I locked onto her, my eyes wanting to pull to the windows as if they had a mind of their own. "I saw a few of your videos online. You do a good job, they're hilarious actually."

"Ugh, it's such a pain in the ass to do it by myself though. I have to use a tripod and record like, triple the amount of footage because for sure some of it will suck." A little twinkle popped into her eye. "I want this video to really catch Mr. Richards' attention. If this internship is gonna be worth anything, he needs to know my name."

"That's Noah's dad, right?"

She nodded. "He's some kind of trillionaire or something. Bought this mountain as a little pet project for Noah, I think. But he owns businesses all over the world. If I can get his attention, maybe I'll be running a social media department for a big multi-national after I graduate."

You wouldn't know it to look at her, but Kayla Yu was as ruthless and cutthroat as they come. She used her physical appearance to skate under the radar. No one suspects the cutesy Asian girl with the bubbly personality would be much trouble. Usually, it was a lesson people only learned once.

I jumped every time the gondola rolled through the support poles, the entire box shaking like it was going to detach from the cable and go flying. Finally, after what seemed to be an eternity, it started to level out. We slowed as it entered an open structure, gliding onto a track that we could step out on. A cute guy in a jacket that looked two sizes too big slid the door open with thunk.

"Hey Kayla. Roughing it outside the lodge today?"

"Oh, you know. I'd rather hang out with manly men who don't need to work in heated offices," she said taking his offered hand. I stood, the car still wobbling beneath my feet. I tightened my grip on the camera bag and stepped out, thankful for solid ground.

"I'm always happy to be in one of your videos if you want," he said too eagerly.

She patted him on the arm and smiled, turning to me. "Alright, let's get started."

It was easily ten degrees colder on the top of the mountain. I'd worn a thick, puffy jacket that came below my ass. Any warmth it gave me was nullified by my thin pants.

We hiked a little way down the flat bit by a trail, stopping at the edge as it dropped away. I chanced a peek over the impossibly steep run and took a few dizzying steps back. How could anyone in their right mind strap a couple sticks to their feet and go down that? All I could imagine was taking a nasty fall, my lifeless body sliding all the way down to the front of the lodge a million feet below.

"Cool! This is perfect. If I interview people here, you can see the mountains in the background right?"

I crouched down to look through the camera, adjusting the focus slightly and gave her a thumbs up. "Looks good." Kayla took out a mirror to fix her hair and makeup. She had a tight white knit cap pulled down, her hair framing her face perfectly. The cold had given her cheeks and nose a pink flush.

As she got ready, I took a minute to take in the scenery. The view was absolutely incredible. We were standing on one of the tallest mountains around, the entire snow-capped range stretching out in front of me. The brilliant blue sky made the whites and greens look even brighter. Taking a deep breath, I understood how this area could get under your skin. What I couldn't understand was how people could just fling themselves over the edge of the trail like it was nothing.

I actually screamed when a skier just casually zoomed past us and disappeared. It was like watching someone jump off a building.

Kayla laughed at me, my eyes filled with terror. “It’s okay. No one accidentally goes down a double diamond run.”

“Do you?” I asked, my eyes still wide. How could even tell which run was which?

“God no, not yet. I’m only up to intermediate. Oh wait! Excuse me? Can I ask you a couple questions for Angel Vista TV?”

Kayla didn’t really need my help. She called people over as they exited the lifts, thrusting a microphone in their faces.

“What’s your favorite dirty ski joke?” she asked, flashing her brilliant smile. I couldn’t believe some of the jokes people delivered. I had to cover my mouth to keep from ruining the audio with my laughter.

“What’s the difference between a ski instructor and God? God doesn’t think he’s a ski instructor.”

“What do snowboarders use as birth control? Their personalities.”

Just as we were about to finish up, she snagged an older woman who looked to be about my grandmother's age. After a brief chat back and forth, Kayla asked for her favorite ski related joke, not even a raunchy one. After a moment's consideration, a wicked smile spread across the old woman's face.

"How many ski instructors does it take to screw in a light bulb?"

"I don't know, how many?" Kayla replied.

"Ski instructors don't screw in light bulbs, dear. They screw in hot tubs." After delivering the punchline, the woman skied off without a word, leaving Kayla laughing appreciatively. She turned back to the camera with a chuckle.

"Well there you have it! Proof that life is not only better, but funnier, on the slopes. I'm Kayla Yu coming to you from beautiful Angel Vista." She smiled for a few more seconds before collapsing in a fit of giggles. I finally let mine loose too. "God, that last woman was perfect! I want to go find her and buy her a drink."

I closed the view on the camera and started to close the tripod. "Honestly, you got some really great stuff. I take it everyone hates ski instructors, ski patrol, and snowboarders."

"It's all in good fun." She blew into her hands,

jumping up and down a little. “Let’s get the fuck inside. It’s freezing up here!”

The ride down in the gondola was much better. I’d lived at sea level my whole life. The mountains were a little overwhelming at first but they were starting to grow on me. Their height was beginning to feel safe, protective.

After dropping off the equipment in her office, Kayla gave me a quick tour of the lodge. High, vaulted ceilings with exposed wooden beams soared over large stone fireplaces and cozy seating areas. The ambiance was warm and inviting, not too different from the cabin I called home for the winter.

As she led me through the main hall, it became obvious the owners were intent on modernizing the lodge. The architecture changed abruptly as we walked through the dining hall. The kitchen surfaces gleamed with shiny stainless steel and dark marble. The walls were no longer a warm brown but an ashy white. It looked modern, like what a millionaire might imagine a cabin should look like.

Kayla suddenly burst to life mid-sentence, beaming at a middle-aged man holding a cup of coffee. “Mr. Roberts! Just the person I was hoping to see.” A man with salt and pepper hair turned toward her bubbly voice and I could tell straight away, this was Noah's father.

"Ms. Yu," he replied coolly, his eyes traveling up and down my body without shame. *I can see where Noah gets it from*, I thought. "And miss…"

"This is my friend Liz. She actually lives at the cabin with us—"

"Ah, Elizabeth Croyden," he said with a knowing nod. I met his cold eyes, trying not to reveal how weirded out I was that he knew my full name. He extended his hand, unnaturally warm from holding the coffee. "After you get settled, I assume you'll be applying for a position here?"

I pulled my hand away and shook my head, forcing a friendly face. "Probably not, no. I'm focusing on my photography this winter."

He smiled at Kayla. "It's a shame. I'd much rather hire from out of state. These locals are an ungrateful bunch." I glanced around, shocked that he didn't even bother lowering his voice but he still continued. "You'd think bringing in millions of additional revenue would come with a little thanks but apparently not." A vein in his temple pulsed slightly but he shook his head. "Anyway."

"I'm just about to upload another video to the website, Mr. Roberts. I'd be happy to stop by your office and show it to you when it's ready," Kayla chimed in.

I stopped short of cringing when he looked at her, nearly licking his lips like a hungry predator. "I look forward to it, Ms. Yu. And I expect you'll both be enjoying the powder day?"

"Oh, I don't ski," I blurted. The innuendo laced conversation had me on edge and wanting to run for the hills. I would've said anything to break up the way he was looking at her.

"No? We'll have to remedy that. Kayla, why don't you take your friend to the rental shop and get her set up, on me of course."

"That's really nice of you, but—"

"I insist. Any friend of Noah's is welcome to ski for free here. It certainly pays be friends with the Roberts family." His voice was warm but the subtext of his words were icy. I felt like he knew everything about me, my full name just the start. Without waiting for a response, he quickly excused himself, reminding Kayla to see him in his office before she left for the day.

I looked to Kayla for some sort of explanation but she only gave me a coy smile. "Come on, at least now I don't have to drive you back to the house."

"I'm pretty sure he knows your name," I said poking her in the ribs.

"Don't I get a say in this?" I moaned, my nerves already jangling.

The entire resort was busy but the rental shop was absolutely heaving. Mid-morning and people were still flowing in, playing hooky from work and school to take advantage of the fresh snow. I dodged out of the way of a couple kids, skis slung over their shoulders and laughing as they ran to the door.

Kayla grabbed my hand and led me through the maze to a harried looking girl giving out equipment receipts. "Emily! It's so crazy in here."

The girl groaned and slumped on the counter. Wisps of blonde hair framed her round, friendly face, pulled loose from running around all morning. "You have *no* idea. Just wait until Christmas. We get a snow like this during Christmas break and it's mayhem."

"Can't wait," Kayla laughed. "Listen, this is my bestie Liz. Mr. Roberts wanted me to hook her up with some rental stuff."

“Yeah, no problem. I need a break from dealing with these little shits.” She held out her hand and smiled. “Hey Liz, great to meet you. What level skier are you?” My fear must’ve been evident because she instantly nodded. “Okay, Level 1 it is. Fill out this form. Don’t lie about your weight, not that you have any reason to,” she muttered sarcastically, “and I’ll be right back.”

“So you’re good?” Kayla asked half way out the door.

“Wait, what? You’re not coming with me?” I was a little embarrassed at the amount of terror I heard in my voice. When I remembered the height of the mountain, I didn’t care.

“I’m supposed to be working,” she giggled. “You’re gonna be fine. Gravity takes care of it all for you.”

“Gravity takes you right off a cliff face,” I cried. I hated showing how terrified I actually was. Damn her for taking me to the top of the mountain before I knew how to ski!

“You’ll be on the bunny slope, stupid. It’s right over there.” She pointed through the rental area to a hill that looked pretty much flat. I watched as a kid took a pretty messy fall right on his face. “That reminds me.” She reached over my arm and checked two boxes on the form. “There.”

“A helmet I can deal with but I’m not taking lessons. I’m done, seriously.” I held up my hands, backing away from the counter.

“Don’t be such a pussy. Everyone is a beginner at some point.”

“Fine. But I’m learning it by myself.”

“You suit yourself,” she replied. “Why don’t we meet in the restaurant around noon for lunch? I can drive you home after that if you want.” By this time, Emily had returned to collect my form. Kayla stuck her bottom lip out and sniffed. “You promised we’d be snow bunnies together, remember? Life experiences, broadening your horizons…”

I scowled, irked that she knew exactly which buttons to press. “I hate you,” I grumbled, hastily writing down my height, weight, and shoe size before I could chicken out.

“Love you, too. See you for lunch. Thanks Emily, I owe you!” She turned quickly with her dark hair spinning behind. Kayla disappeared into the crowd and essentially left me to die. Nice.

No one told me the hardest part about skiing was just getting the equipment on. Helmet, skis, poles, all good, but the boots! Whoever designed those things was a straight up sadist. It took ten minutes to get one foot inside. Emily was such a sweetheart and stuck with me, kneeling in front as I grunted in frustration.

"All you have to do is slide your toe in and stand up, okay? You can hold onto my shoulders."

"I'm telling you, they're still too small," I complained. I watched a couple snowboarders walk by in envy. *Why the hell did I say skiing?*

"I'm the professional here. Stand and put all your weight on your leg."

My foot was wedged in the boot like I was wearing the tallest stiletto in the world. Just when I was about to declare that I was a lost cause, my heel slipped down and hit the bottom of the boot with a thud.

"Oh!" I cried, falling back onto the bench. "I'm in!"

"That's what he said," Emily snickered. A few teenage girls overheard and broke into a fit of giggles but I didn't care. I had a boot on, a real ski boot! "One down, one to go. This one'll be easier." True to her word, Emily got me into the last boot but she didn't warn me how horrible they were to walk in. After tightening the buckles, she explained, "You walk heel, toe, heel, toe." When I tried it, it went more like, *heel-slam-scrape-swear*.

Once I sort of got the hang of it, I thanked her

profusely for helping and shooed her away. Sitting on the bench in the middle of all the craziness, I gave myself a little pep talk. *You can do it. You can do whatever you put your mind to and right now, you're putting your mind to this. Even if you fall and make a complete ass out of yourself, you at least have to try. Besides, Mom was a natural and you will be too.*

I tightened the strap around my chin, gathered my poles and skis, and went *heel-slam, heel-slam* all the way to the base of the bunny slope. For the sake of brevity and my pride, let's just say that after a little while, I managed to get everything in place and my body at the top of the hill. Sweaty, breathless, and frustrated and I hadn't even started yet.

"God, this looks a lot steeper from up here," I whispered to myself. A kid no older than four or five stepped off the magic carpet and zipped past me down the slope, his dad following behind with a camera. "You gotta be kidding me…"

After watching a few others around me, I thought I had the basic idea. Turning seemed to be the most difficult part, so I pointed my skis nearly parallel with the bottom of the slope and started sliding. I slid across the entire width of the slope before I realized I was running out of space. Thankfully, I was going so slowly I only had to slam my poles in the ground before I tangled myself in the orange safety net. I gingerly picked up one ski and pointed it back in the direction from which I'd just come, holding onto my staked poles for dear life. Thanking my diligent yoga practice, I stood with my feet pointing in opposite directions with just a tiny bit of discomfort. I lifted my other ski and after a slight wobble, was safely on back on two feet, everything facing the same way.

I slowly skidded back across the slope, my confidence soaring with every slippery inch. My nerves were on edge as I approached the other side, nearly two-thirds the way there. I was so focused on planning my turn I didn't think to look at who might be approaching from the slope above. Might as well be wearing blinders for all the attention I was giving the rest of the world.

"Bail, bail!" I heard a deep male voice urgently yell. I turned my head for a fraction of a second to see a terrified kid barreling at me at lightning speed. Not that I had any idea what to do, I didn't have any time to react. The kid scrunched his face up and fell, but he'd made his decision far too late. The speed carried him straight into my ankles, bowling me over like a pin. I managed to throw myself to the side and avoided crushing the poor kid, but that only landed me right on his hard plastic boots. Pain shot through my hip and I knew instantly I'd be sporting a beautiful purple bruise for weeks.

"I'm so sorry," the boy said meekly.

I rolled off him with a groan and waved a gloved hand at him. "Totally my fault." Although hardly an injury worth mentioning, the pain was nauseating, the same as a stubbed toe. As I tried to swallow back my breakfast, I heard the quick swish of snow behind me. I sat up, leaning back on my hands. My legs were stuck in awkward angles because my boots hadn't popped out when I crashed. I tried to push through the pain and remember Emily's instructions on how to get out of the bindings.

"Hey buddy, are you alright?" A guy skied down, helped the kid up and gave him a good once over. The way I was sitting, I could only listen. "Aw, you're good. Looked like a pretty awesome wreck."

"Yeah?" the boy said eagerly.

"Totally. You're good to go. I think your sister is waiting for you down there."

I watched as the little speed bump skied down the hill.

I breathed slowly, waiting for the sick feeling to finally pass and the guy to carry on. But he didn't.

"Lady, I know you're new but you should really look where you're going."

My chest tightening with barely suppressed anger, I tried to turn and look at him. Shielding my eyes from the sun, his face was mostly obscured by a pair of big orange goggles. "Ah, so you're the guy who's teaching blind kids to ski? I'm pretty sure he could've seen me just as easily. Accidents happen."

He opened his mouth to speak and then groaned. He shook his head, dropping his chin to his chest. "Ah shit. Why can't I talk to you without it turning into some huge thing?"

I was too fired up to recognize his voice. I'd already climbed onto my indignant horse and was waving my bitchy banner. "I don't know what the hell that's supposed to mean. As far as I can tell, that kid is the only one who walked away from this crash unscathed. There should be some kind of capacity out here. It's dangerous and—" As I was speaking, he pulled off his goggles, the brightest green eyes gazing down at me. Not a whole lot can stop me once I start ranting but those eyes…my heart fluttered and the nausea returned. Why *couldn't* we meet without fighting?

"Liz, I really want to explain about the other night—"

"Bryan, I thought you worked—"

"I do. Powder day, you know. I was just out here testing out some new equipment." He tapped a ski with his pole, a bright red and white pair that made my rentals look like a Fiat to his Ferrari.

I suddenly felt really odd talking to him while sitting at waist height, the sun blinding me. I tried to push myself up but flopped back down on my ass in a heap.

"Do you want some help?" he asked. If I'd detected even an ounce of laughter in his voice, I would've declined. Instead, I held up my arm.

"Yes, please."

He reached out but hesitated, a small curl forming at the corner of his mouth. "Do I have permission to touch you?"

I rolled my eyes but bit my tongue. After the way I'd reacted the first time we met, I deserved that. "You may touch my hands and arms. I'll have to decide about the rest later on."

With a laugh, he bent and scooped me up. I was surprised at his strength. While muscular, he was quite lean. I didn't expect him to lift me so easily. It was difficult to maintain my dignity while fighting to stay upright. With a firm grip on his shoulder, I tried to regain my balance, nearly falling once again. With a quick move, he caught me in his arms, our faces only inches apart.

"You okay?" he whispered with lips I needed to feel against mine.

My eyes flickered from his mouth to his eyes, breath catching in my throat. "I'm good. Good."

We stayed that way for a moment, that agonizing space between not kissing and kissing. I had to remind myself I was still upset with the guy. No matter how good looking he was, he'd been incredibly rude…but just one kiss couldn't hurt. Just as my resolve weakened, he glanced away, deliberately breaking the connection.

"I still have another fifteen minutes with this gear and then I'm done for the day. If you stick around, I'd like to buy you a cup of coffee and apologize for the other night." His expression was so earnest. Any other guy, I would've told him to fuck off but I still hadn't figured him out yet. He still had a slim chance to get back in my good books. Old Liz wouldn't give a guy a second chance, so I figured New Liz should.

"Okay. I'll meet you in there. I think I need to get

some ice for my ass anyway," I said with a grimace. I almost smiled at the relief in his face but kept my face stern.

"Good! I'll see you in there. Great! Thank you." He kissed me quickly on the cheek, skiing away before I had a chance to react. Even though I didn't want to admit it to myself, that kiss made me feel as giddy as a junior high girl at her first dance. My cheek tingled all the way down the slope. And while it might've taken me forever to get down, I didn't fall once. Bonus points for not killing any small children on the way!

Bryan

Liz didn't hate me! My exhilaration practically floated me down the bunny slope. I felt like I'd just asked out a girl for the first time and I wasn't rejected. I glanced back up the hill to see Liz nearly fall over as she retrieved her poles. I didn't want to show up a sweaty mess but I wasn't going to have time to take another run before having to return the skis to the pro shop. I was able to run to my locker, change my shirt, and splash a little water on my face. As luck would have it, I found a small bottle of cologne on the bottom of my bag, which I hastily sprayed before rushing back to the dining room.

I stood in the doorway and scanned the room, finally spotting her sitting in a plush chair near the fireplace. I paused, just wanting to look at her for a moment. She sat with her legs crossed, her beautiful pale skin was flushed from exertion and the cold. She idly ran her fingers through her brown hair, looking around the room, presumably for me. With an unfamiliar knot in my stomach, I finally found my balls and walked over to her.

"Hi again," I managed as our eyes met. She had the most piercing eyes I'd ever seen. In fact, I remember little else from the other night in the bar than her eyes and her laugh. "Can I get you a coffee?"

"I'll decide that after I hear your explanation," she replied coolly. She glanced at the empty seat beside, separated by a small, round table.

As I sat, I realized I was trembling with nerves. I hadn't exactly thought through what I was going to say. I'd been too excited that she hadn't slapped me. I cleared my throat as she looked on expectantly. *Maybe she isn't as pleased to see me as I thought?*

I sat forward in the seat, my elbows resting on my knees, fingers clasped. I stared at my hands as I began to speak. "I don't really remember everything that happened the other night, but I do remember I did something to upset you."

She scoffed and folded her arms over her chest. "You could say that." She flicked her head slightly, clearing the hair from her eyes. God, those eyes could make or break me…

I took a deep breath and nodded. "We don't have to go over it. I'm sure whatever I said was really insensitive for you to leave like that, but I wanted to say—"

"You asked me if my back hurt because my tits are so big." Liz arched her eyebrow, her foot starting to shake in annoyance. She'd spoken loudly enough a few heads turned to look.

"Jesus, I'm so sorry," I groaned, wiping my face with my hand. Had I actually been that rude? How was she still talking to me? I couldn't meet her eye as I continued. "This isn't an excuse, by any means, but…I'm on medication that apparently interacts—okay, that's a little vague. That makes me sound crazy or something. I'm on a new pain medication that doesn't mix well with alcohol, I guess. I had a little too much to drink and it…" I glanced up at her unimpressed expression and sighed. "I was in an accident a couple years ago."

"I know," she said quickly.

"You know?" Fuck, she knows who I am after all. I braced myself. If there's anything worse than The Squint or The Look, it's The Remembering. *Oh, how terrible. I remember when I saw that crash on TV…I remember seeing your fiance on the front of Gossip Magazine.*

“You took your shirt off when I put you to bed. It’s not hard to notice all the scars.” I must’ve winced at that because she quickly added, “I mean, they aren’t *bad.* I just saw them and figured something bad had happened.” A silence fell between us and I wanted to sink into my chair and disappear into the floor. She pursed her lips slighty and chuckled. “Shit, I’m sorry. Now I’m the one being rude. I guess we’re even now.”

I loved the way her cheeks dimpled when she smiled. I was so happy she was smiling again, I couldn’t help grinning back at her. The whole situation was incredibly embarrassing, I felt completely rocked back on my heels. Whatever confidence I’d regained talking to her at the bar had been wiped back to zero by my behavior.

“So, can I buy you that coffee now?” I asked, my heart pounding as I approached the last hurdle. *Please say yes, please…*

“I suppose…” she replied with a sideways glance.

“That was just the explanation, I still have to apologize. The coffee’s just the first part,” I said as I stood, walking away before she could reject the offer.

With the awkwardness out of the way, our conversation flowed. I discovered she was an only child from all over but mainly North Carolina, born and raised on military bases, her dad was a Marine. She told me she was taking the spring semester off to clear her head. We kept the conversation light but I could feel some real weight hiding behind her comments. I noticed that she talked about her dad all the time but never her mom. And for some reason I just wasn't buying the story about school being too stressful. If I'm honest, I was a little miffed that she wasn't telling me the entire truth but I had to remind myself that neither was I. Lying by omission had become almost a hobby of mine. Plus, we were practically strangers. She was under no obligation to tell me anything she didn't want to.

We were there for almost an hour talking, laughing. I fell in love with the way she held her coffee with both hands, closing her eyes nearly every time she took a sip. The whole lodge disappeared, leaving me and Liz and the crackling fire. It was mystifying. Nothing we said, nothing we did could explain the draw I felt towards her. On the surface, our conversation wasn't anything special but there's nothing in the world that could've pulled my attention away from her.

"So, what about you?" she asked setting her empty coffee cup down. She uncrossed and crossed her legs so she was leaning closer.

“What about me?” I knew I could play coy for only so long. At least at this point I could pass it off as flirting.

“Siblings? Parents?” She traced the edge of the mug with her finger, her gaze down.

“Brother, younger, lives in California with my mom.”

“Parents divorced?” she asked, still not looking up.

I don’t know why I said it. Maybe a part of me was ready to start talking about it. Maybe I wanted to pull whatever it was she was hiding out. Maybe I just wanted to see her eyes again. I cleared my throat and spoke softly. “Um, no. Actually, my dad died two years ago.”

Her eyes flicked up to mine, filled with sympathy. “I’m sorry, I know how hard that is.” It was that moment I knew her mother was gone as well. I reached for her hand, my calluses rubbing against her soft skin.

“It’s okay. I don’t talk about it much, but it’s gets easier, ya know?” She squeezed my hand in response, nodding. We could see the loss reflected in each other. I found real comfort in that, connecting with someone outside my family about my dad. It was the last thing I expected to happen when I asked her to join me in the lodge.

“Can I ask you a personal question? And you can totally say no, I don’t mind.” Her blue eyes glittered, flitting back and forth between mine.

“Absolutely.” I’d answer anything if meant I could keep holding her hand.

Liz nibbled the edge of her bottom lip, searching for the right way to phrase her question. “How did get all those…I mean, shit. What kind of accident was it?”

I studied her face as I studied myself. Was I really ready to go into all that? I enjoyed her knowing me as “Bryan,” not “The Blizzard.” I’m sure she’d Google me before long and learn everything, so should I risk the lie? Did I even have it all straight in my head—

“Car crash,” I heard myself say. Was a half-truth still a lie?

“Ah,” she replied, her expression changing slightly. “I could’ve sworn you were a soldier.”

My laugh surprised her. “Seriously? I don’t think I’ve ever gotten that one before.” She dropped her hand from mine with a shrug. Was she disappointed?

“You just reminded me of a lot of guys I knew back home, that’s all. I guess trauma is trauma, whether you get it in the desert or the side of the road.” I wasn’t sure what to say to that. She’d managed to see right through me. Was I that transparent or was she that good?

She gasped and grabbed her pocket, eyes wide. “Oh shit, that scared me! Phone’s on vibrate. Hold on.” Leaning away slightly to answer the call, “Hey. Yes I’m alive, you bitch,” she rolled her eyes at me. “Yeah? Okay, I’ll be here. I’m by the big fire in the middle. Alright.” She slipped the phone back into her pocket. “That was my friend, we’re meeting for lunch. I can’t believe how late it’s gotten,” she said staring at the clock on her phone.

That made me smile. I was glad time had gone too quickly for her as well. “Sounds good. Except,” I paused, giving her a coy smile, “I haven’t properly thanked you for taking care of me and my truck the other day.”

“Not a big deal, really,” she said with a wave of the hand. “Trust me, I know how booze can fuck with drugs.”

“Really. I feel like I owe you. I was thinking, if you’re up for it, I could teach you how to ski? Could even do it this afternoon, assuming you haven’t booked lessons.” I did my best to appear casual but I was dying inside. If she said no to this, I’d have to come up with some other way of getting her alone. My confidence wasn’t ready to ask anyone out to dinner.

“That’s really nice of you, but—”

I sighed, clapping my hands together quietly. “You’re

gonna make me say it? Alright, I'll say it." Liz's eyebrows furrowed, the bridge of her nose crinkling slightly. "I feel like it's my obligation to give you lessons, if not for your safety, then for theirs," I gestured around the lodge. "You're a bit of a hazard."

"Hey!" she said, giving my shoulder a playful slap. "That fucking kid came out of nowhere."

"He was wearing a bright orange jump suit," I replied, trying to hold back my laughter.

Liz sighed, tilting her head as she smiled at me. I wasn't sure what was holding her back, most people would jump at the offer of free lessons. "I kind of wanted to teach myself. I think I'll be a natural."

"Nope." The quickness of my reply earned another slap, harder this time. "I'm not saying you can't learn, jeez!"

"Fine, fine. I accept. Do you think we could do it today, though? I already have all my stuff rented and I'm *not* going through that whole process again. You have no idea how long it took to get these fucking things on," she said waggling her boot at me.

"Oh shit," I exclaimed. "I didn't realize you were still locked in." I crouched down in front of her and loosened the buckles and straps, pulling the boot tongue open. "Is that better?" I asked, looking up at her.

She exhaled in relief. "So much better. I didn't realize you could do that! I thought I was going to loose circulation."

It took me a moment to realize I had a hand on her calf, the warmth of her leg radiating through her pants. I kept my gaze firm, willing at least a piece of The Blizzard to the surface. "Let me put my number in your phone. Give me a call when you're done with lunch and we'll meet up."

Liz swallowed and reached into her pocket. I stood as smoothly as I could, trying to hide the grimace as my knee locked up. Rather than type my number in her contacts list, I dialed myself. That way I'd at least have her number if she bailed on me. Even though I'd been pretty lucky so far, I wasn't sure how long fate was going to keep throwing us together.

"There." Our fingers brushed as I handed the phone back, sending a little zing through my arm. "I really need to get going, but I'll hopefully see you in an hour or two, okay?"

"Yeah, cool," she nodded. "See you later."

I left before I completely ruined whatever charm I'd managed to lay on her. She actually seemed flustered when I touched her! Now, I just had an hour to kill while I nervously awaited her call.

After leaving Liz, I'd grabbed a sandwich and found a quiet place to obsessively check the time on my phone for the next hour. When she called, it took every ounce of strength to remain cool. A half hour into the lesson and I knew there was no point fighting it. I was crushing on this girl big time. Everything she did was either cute or sexy or hilarious, sometimes an amazing combination of all three. Even though she was focused on learning how to ski, I was getting some great vibes from her. I didn't feel like it was too much of a risk to try a few moves out, rusty or not.

There are appropriate ways of teaching someone how to ski and then there are, well…techniques that, while perfectly valid, offer more opportunities for contact. Do you have press your groin against someone's ass in order to teach them how to swing a golf club? Absolutely not. Do you have to pin a girl against the table from behind when teaching her how to shoot pool? Of course not, but in the right circumstances, it makes it a hell of a lot more fun.

"You're gonna laugh at this one," I said as we slid off the magic carpet. She shuffled along behind me, struggling to move forward on the flat surface.

"Okay," she replied dubiously. I'd noticed she bit her lower lip a lot when she was concentrating. I couldn't stop looking at her mouth, wanting nothing more than to feel her swollen lips against mine.

"This'll help you feel what it's like to turn all the way down the mountain, okay? With my help, you're going to start stringing turns together."

"I'm missing the punchline. This sounds scary, not funny."

"Because," I said as I sidestepped behind her, "we're going to go down together, like this." I put my skis on either side of hers, the length of my legs making it possible to press against the outside of her boots. Placing my hands on her waist, I demonstrated how I was going to guide us down. Again, not the only way I could teach her how to turn but definitely the most fun.

She glanced over her shoulder. "Did I give you permission to do that?"

"When you agreed to take lessons from me."

"You're fucking with me, right?" I felt a blush rise in my cheeks but stuck with it. "Nope, this'll provide the muscle memory you need to get over your fear of turns."

"And what's that digging into my ass?" she said,

wiggling her backside against my groin. I nearly moaned with the contact, my cock stirring to life, but I thought fast.

"Oh, that? Just the handle of my pole." Thankfully, it was half true. I waved the pole to the side, satisfied I'd managed to keep the upper hand on that one. Now that I had a growing bulge in my pants, I'd have to keep the contact to a minimum. "Are you ready?"

"Wait," she stiffened as I started to push us forward. "Why haven't I seen anyone else doing this out here?"

"It's a special technique of mine."

She snorted. "Yeah? Were you doing this special technique with orange jumpsuit kid?"

"He already knew how to turn." She huffed in response, still not convinced. "Don't you trust me?" I prodded. Our eyes connected, my breath coming out in short clouds. Every time I looked at it her, it was like I was seeing her for the first time.

"Jury's still out on that one," she said with a squint.

"Ouch, alright. Fair enough," I said stepping back. "The deal was that I'll teach you how to ski. I'll just go find you another instructor you can trust."

"Oh for fuck's sake, get back here," she said, grabbing my hand. I slid back into place with a little too much excitement. Whether she felt exactly how excited I was, she didn't say, but it was obvious. I took a deep breath and although she was looking downhill, I could tell by her profile she was smiling.

"Okay, we'll take it slowly. I'll do most of the work and I promise I won't let you fall."

The crowds on the slope were thinning. On big powder days, people liked to get in early to grab the virgin snow. By now, they were tired, hungry, and depressed about having to go to work tomorrow. Only so many sick days in a year.

I led us down the bunny slope with wide, looping turns. We criss-crossed the trail on a nearly horizontal path, taking it slow and easy. Every time I initiated the turn, Liz released a tiny squeal as we picked up speed.

"That's the hardest part about turns," I said in her ear. "You have to get comfortable with giving yourself over to gravity. It'll pull you downhill but you start to trust that you're able to break away whenever you want."

Even through the gloves and layers, I could feel the tense muscles of her hips working. I mentally stripped the layers away, imagining her on top of me, my hands on her naked hips as she writhed and twisted—

"You okay back there, instructor?" she asked, pressing

her ass into my cock. "You gotta watch where that pole's poking."

Still flustered from the intense image of her, I had no witty response. I opted to stay as professional as I could, under the circumstances. "We're approaching the end, so we'll take one final turn and then wedge our skis like I showed you, remember?"

We executed the turn perfectly, our bodies moving in sync. I pushed the tips of my skis together, forcing hers in turn. The wedge shape was the common way beginners learned to slow and stop. Unfortunately, the position lit waves of fiery pain up my knee and hip. I was coated with a thin sheet of sweat within seconds, gritting my teeth to keep from crying out. As we slowed, I allowed her to drift away and come to a stop on her own.

Liz threw her arms up in the air, poles dangling from her wrists, and cheered. "I did it! I actually fucking did it." I glided alongside her, planting my poles in the snow so I'd stop without having to use my sore leg.

"Yes you did," I grinned at her. I was about to suggest we call it a day when she spoke up.

"Do you think I can go down that one over there?" I followed her finger to the West Slope. Still a beginner's level, it was twice as long and a bit steeper. The bright flood lights flickered on, bathing the white snow in an orange hue.

"Are you sure?" I asked. "You've done really well today, I thought maybe we—"

"I'm sure." She set her jaw and stared at me intently. "I don't want my first day to just be on the bunny slope. Please?"

"You'll have to do it yourself. I can't follow behind like we just did." I loved how into it she was but I wasn't sure she was ready to advance to the next slope.

She nodded eagerly. "That's exactly what I was hoping for."

A few minutes later, we were sharing a chair to the top of the West Slope. I pulled the safety bar down and showed her how to balance her skis on the metal below. She rocked back in the seat, eyes locked on the cable above our heads.

"Damnit, why do these things have to be so high up?" she muttered to herself. Liz took a few deep breaths, her cheeks puffing out as she slowly exhaled. "Maybe this was a bad idea."

"Don't say that. You're kicking ass." A memory of my dad popped into my mind. Rather than pushing it away like I always did, I embraced it. Pointing to the run we were about to go down, I continued, "Take a look at the trail. Imagine yourself standing on top of it, about to go down."

Liz dropped her gaze to me, fear and doubt evident in her eyes. "I can't, I really can't. This was so stupid."

"Just look," I said firmly. I carried on as she slowly turned away from me. "Imagine yourself standing at the top, like a little figure up there," I pointed. "Picture yourself going down the run. Map the path you'd take with your eyes, the broad turns you'd take—"

"The place where I face plant and slide all the way down."

"Stop, I'm serious. Positive visualization is a powerful thing. My dad taught me when I was little, just like this." Liz fell quiet. There was no way she could've known how rare it was for me to talk about him, but I was glad she was there to listen. "It's almost like you're holding a figurine of yourself, like this!" We watched as a snowboarder came flying over the edge, obviously continuing his run from the top of the mountain judging by his speed. I leaned over her and pinched my fingers together, the perspective making it look like I was guiding him down the mountain by hand.

Liz tensed as the chair rocked with my movement, grabbing my bicep. "Sorry," she said with embarrassment.

"Don't be." My chest swelled when I realized she wasn't going to remove her hand. "So, in your mind, you're flying down the run but at the same time, you're sitting here trying to imagine what it'd feel like. What muscles would you use, how you'd shift and lean, stuff like that. I don't expect you to know how to do that yet, but you'll get there."

She smiled at me warmly, giving my arm a little squeeze. "Your dad taught you that?"

The memory still felt raw but for some reason, it didn't sting so badly when she was with me. I nodded tightly. "Actually, it was on that lift over there, before they turned it into the gondolas. It was my first trip to the top and he told me the same thing."

A comfortable silence fell between us. The snow and mountains always brought me peace, exactly what I'd been looking for when I packed up and left for Tellure Hollow. I wasn't expecting to find someone I could feel just as peaceful with, especially so quickly. I looked at her out of the corner of my eye. There was something about her, about the two of us, that matched on a cellular level.

"What?" she giggled a little self-consciously.

"We're at the top," I replied, tilting my head towards the fast approaching end. Her grip on my arm strengthened as I lifted the safety bar. “It’s simple. Keep your tips pointed up and scoot your ass to the edge of the seat. When the snow rises to meet you, just stand up.”

I thought she was going to chew her bottom lip off completely. “Okay. Can I still hold onto you?”

“Absolutely.” Oh yeah, I had it bad for this girl. This was trouble.

I gave the liftie a quick nod to let him know I had a beginner with me. The last thing I wanted was Liz getting whacked on the back of the head by the chair or something stupid. Firmly, I repeated the same instructions, the exit gently rising to meet our skis. I stood quickly, nearly yanking her to her feet, and let the momentum of the hill carry us down.

“Shit, shit, shit, shit,” she cried, clutching at my arm. I had to hold her up but we both made it to the bottom without falling.

“See? Not hard at all,” I said, patting her hand with mine.

“Piece of cake.” I chuckled as she rolled her eyes and exhaled dramatically.

The snow on this side of the mountain was a little more choppy. The sun softened it during the day and now as the temperature dropped, the carved snow was turning to icy granules. It wasn't anything I'd think twice about, but for a beginner, it was night and day compared to powder. I pushed forward to the crest of the hill and looked back to watch Liz shamble over. She released a string of obscenities as she drew close.

"That is *so* steep. I can't do that, I can't," she insisted.

"You absolutely can. Just keep your skis in a wedge and you won't go fast at all. I'm going to go down a little bit ahead of you. I want you to concentrate on following my tracks." She looked terrified, her eyes practically pleading me for another way down. I rubbed her back and leaned close, the smell of her sweat and shampoo flooding my senses. "You've fucking got this, Liz. Trust me."

Staring down the hill, she nodded, convincing herself of that truth. When our eyes met, I thought for a second she might kiss me. Maybe she would've if she hadn't been afraid I was leading her to her death.

"I trust you," she said softly.

"Good. First part is the steepest then it levels out like the bunny slope. You ready?"

She squeezed her eyes shut and nodded. "Yes."

"You'll have to open your eyes first," I joked.

Laughing at the glare she shot me, I pushed off.

Even though the pain was excruciating, I pointed my tips together and took wide, serpentine turns. I kept an eye on Liz over my shoulder. Her mouth was moving, and even though I was too far away to hear, I was sure she was cursing up a storm. Her eyes glued to the tracks I was leaving, she roughly followed the same path down. Just as I'd hoped, her concentration broke through any fear she had about pointing downhill.

"You're doing great," I yelled. When she glanced up at my voice, I knew she was in for a tumble. As she lifted her head and lost concentration, her left tip crossed over her right, catching on a patch of snow.

"Shit!" she yelled as she fell, flinging her arms out to brace herself. A ski popped free from her boot as she collided with the ground. Luckily, she hadn't been going too fast. I collected the loose ski and quickly climbed the hill, my leg and ass muscles screaming in protest. She sat up as I approached.

"Sorry, instructor's curse. I shouldn't have said anything. Are you alright?" I asked tentatively, holding a hand out. She squinted at me before taking it.

"How many ski instructors does it take to put in a

lightbulb?"

I laughed and shook my head. "I don't know, how many?" She grabbed my hand and I pulled her up. Standing downslope, we were now eye-level.

"Eleven. One to put it in and ten to analyzing the turning."

A broad smile spread across my face as I dropped her ski down. She braced herself on my shoulder as she stepped back into the bindings, the ski clicking back into place. "That's a good one, actually. Hadn't heard it in a while. You good to go?" She nodded curtly. I pointed downhill as I spoke. "You see how it levels out there? Watch me go down, watch how my body leans and then follow my tracks."

I stepped back and continued the painful wedge down the rest of the first hill, acutely aware of her eyes on my body. I allowed myself to pick up a little speed towards the flat and shifted my weight, coming to a skate stop in a spray of snow. Waving my hands above my head, I signaled for her to follow.

Tentatively, carefully, she traced my tracks, gaining confidence with every turn. The fall had obviously shaken away a lot of her fear. I grew tense as I noticed she was picking up speed, not quite out of control, but flirting with it.

As she rounded the last curve, I was fully nervous.

"Wedge, wedge!" She headed straight for me. I spread my legs wide, bracing to catch her. Liz veered off at the last second, kicking her heels out in a textbook skate stop, coming to a halt just before the tips of my skis. She showered my lower half with granular snow, grinning at my surprise.

"Isn't that how you did it?" she said with practiced innocence.

I nodded appreciatively, side stepping closer. "Maybe you are a natural."

"I told you I was. I knew—" she stumbled as she tried to step closer, falling into me. I moved in time, barely catching her under the arms.

It happened so quickly, but later I'd run it over and over in my mind. Liz steadied herself, hands on my shoulders, eyes gazing at my mouth. She bit her lower lip for a second before kissing me, her mouth hot and intense against mine. The kiss lasted only a moment but I savored it. She pulled away, scanning my face for a reaction.

Still in my arms, she looked up into my eyes. "We're having a party tomorrow night. You should come," she whispered.

“I—yeah, sure. Love to,” I stammered.

“Good,” she replied. Her eyes darted to my mouth as if she wanted to kiss me again, but she pulled herself upright. “Now, let’s get off this fucking mountain and get a drink. My ass is sore.”

“Say it again,” she giggled, leaning closer. A waft of her perfume floated towards me.

“Après-ski.” I wet my lips and enunciated the word. “*Ah-pray*. It’s French,” I smiled.

“And what does it mean?” She looked at me sideways as she sipped her brandy.

I gestured to the bar, to all the people sitting around us. “This. It means, ‘after skiing’ and some people wrap their whole lives around it. Every mountain has a little group of people who don’t ski but just chill out in the bars and restaurants.”

“Like groupies,” she laughed, tossing her hair back. “For someone who just got into town, you know a lot about this place.”

I shrugged, letting the alcohol warm my throat and

chest. “I kind of grew up around ski resorts.” Technically true.

We were sitting on a plush sofa at the far end of the room. I’d slung my arm over the back casually which Liz had slowly but surely slid beneath. She was now close enough our knees touched. “So, you started skiing when you were little?”

I pressed my knee against her a bit, craving even more contact. “Yeah. Pretty much been skiing my whole life. My dad taught me and my brother before we were five.” I thought about the photo in the album of dad skiing behind me, holding me with the straps.

“And that’s why you came here? So you could ski?”

“Mmmhmm,” It was true…just not completely true. I still wasn’t entirely sure why I’d come to Tellure Hollow. “What about you?” I asked, my fingers grazing her shoulder from above. “What made you want to come here?”

She shrugged, the foot on her crossed leg started to waggle. “Kayla. Well, Kayla and my mom. She loved to ski but since we lived in North Carolina, we never got to go.” She’d managed to inch so close she had to look up into my eyes. “How do you think I did today?”

With a little liquid courage to bolster me, I took a deep

breath. I slid my hand up to the side of her jaw, her hair wrapping around my fingers. I didn't answer her question, my thought tumbling out in its place. "You're incredible." Our lips hovered a fraction apart, noses grazing the skin of our cheeks, the sexual tension almost too much to take.

Liz nibbled her bottom lip before plunging forward, her mouth hot against mine. It was like an explosion went off inside me at the contact. She slid into the crook of my arm, pressing her warm body against mine. The world vanished, my past disappeared. All that mattered was her. Her lips, her scent, her everything. It made every other kiss I'd ever had pale in comparison. I was taken aback by the heat in her eyes when we pulled apart. For a moment, I thought she might tackle me right there. Instead, she took a deep breath and slid back a bit.

"I think I should probably go before I get myself into trouble," she smiled demurely. "You are coming to the party tomorrow night, right?"

"Try to stop me," I smiled.

Liz

I love days that end differently than you expected them to. Never in a million years would I have thought I'd be spending the afternoon with Bryan Marsh, certainly not after the way we'd left things. With all the fresh air, the brandy we had in the lodge after the lesson ended, the kiss…I was buzzing. I was in a blissful, happy place as Kayla pulled the Jeep into the driveway. The cabin glowed in the gloomy night, warm and inviting. A light snow fell, dusting the steps so our shoes left prints as we ascended.

Kayla and I planned what we were going to make for dinner as we kicked off our boots. I immediately spotted Noah in the kitchen, his back turned towards us. Kayla frowned at me.

"Great, maybe we should just skip it. Can't you two just make up? For me?" I hadn't seen Noah much since the altercation, but the strain between us was close to unbearable. I knew it was making everyone in the house uncomfortable and after making up with Bryan, I figured I could swallow my pride and apologize for the sake of peace.

I nodded as I headed for the kitchen. “No, it’s alright,” I said waving her away. “Noah? Can I talk to you in private for a sec?”

He turned, a bottle of open wine in his hand, a single empty glass sat on the counter. His expression was tight, sizing me up. The bruise on the side of his face had faded to a sickly brown. “Sure.” How he managed to fill so much sarcasm into one word was beyond me, but I stamped down my annoyance. He returned the bottle to the counter with a sigh and headed towards me.

It’s amazing how personality accounts for so much of a person’s attractiveness. If he’d been kind, his brown eyes might have seemed warm. If he’d smiled more, his face wouldn’t have appeared as harsh and angular. I pushed the thought from my mind, leading him into the hallway.

I forced myself to look him the eye. “We didn’t get really get started on the best foot, did we?”

Noah gritted his teeth, obviously biting back some snarky comment. “Not exactly.”

“I was kind of hoping, if you want, we could start over.” If it meant keeping the peace, I was willing to play the coy little girl for him. Guys like Noah enjoyed feeling superior to women. "I know if you give me another chance, we'll be friends. Kayla and I are practically sisters and I know you love her." I gave him my best smile, tilting my chin down and gazing up through my eyelashes.

"I wouldn't say love..." His expression hadn't changed, but I could tell his resolve was weakening.

"Please? I've really hated the tension between us. It'd mean a lot to me." The way he looked at me made me want to shiver, like I was a bug underfoot, but I held fast. I didn't bat my eyelashes at him but I wasn't far off. Finally, the mask cracked and he smiled.

"Of course. Nothing would make me happier." Noah offered his hand which I took demurely. He lifted it to his mouth, twisted my arm around so he could kiss my wrist. Every instinct in my body screamed in disgust. He glanced up at me as his lips touched my skin. I let it happen, a stupid, fake smile plastered to my face. I think I was in such shock, I didn't know what else to do. "Do you drink wine?" I nodded in response, at a total loss for words. "I'll pour you a glass."

As I watched him disappear around the corner, something my dad had always told me popped into my head. He'd always told me that men fell into one of two categories.

Some men are bulldogs; hot-blooded, quick to anger, quick to cool. Bulldogs can be fiercely loyal and unless you mistreat them, they'll never turn on you. According to my dad, the men you had to look out for were the snakes. These cold-blooded creatures would plot, hide their anger, plan their strike. Snakes have no allegiance but to themselves. *He's a snake if I've ever met one,* I thought looking at the back of Noah's head.

Kayla and Noah were talking when I returned to the kitchen. He poured the deep burgundy wine into a glass and handed it to me while he spoke. "So, do you like to party Liz?"

Kayla chuckled and glanced at me. "Depends what you mean by party."

"Coke, molly, you know, fucking party." He took a sip of wine, making a gross smack as he swallowed. "I swear, I wouldn't have been able to finish my MBA without my roommate's Ritalin prescription."

Ever since Rick had gotten busted, even talking about drugs made me feel so uncomfortable. It was a world I'd been thrust into so quickly my head was still spinning. Kayla simply saw it as another business opportunity, a product that had a demand and she was willing to distribute.

"Lizzy hasn't touched the stuff in a year and I don't do coke, but you know me. I love MDMA if the mood's right." She flipped her hair over her shoulder with wink.

"We'll have to make sure our guy has plenty for tomorrow then. We'll have a big candy dish of it for everyone."

I shimmied up on the counter, my heels whacking against the cupboard doors. They seemed happy to trade drug stories while Kayla made dinner, allowing my mind to wander back to Bryan. My heart leapt with excitement as I realized the party was essentially our first date. Unless the lesson could've been? It was supposed to be his apology…but then I went and kissed him. Having drinks in the lodge, was that a date? *Shit, how does anyone keep track of this stuff?*

Thoughts of Bryan swirled through my mind, keeping me in my happy daze through dinner. I excused myself and retreated to my bedroom when Kayla and Noah started getting a little too touchy-feely. I'm not much for audience participation.

I switched on the shower, waiting until the windows were fully fogged before undressing. I stepped under the hot water as it cascaded from the waterfall fixture, letting it flow over me. I thought of Bryan. It soaked the chill from my bones and soothed my muscles. Muscles I never knew I *had* ached. At least, if I stuck with the skiing, my legs and ass would be fantastic. As I soaped up, I noticed a bright purple bruise spread across my hip, my punishment for landing on the orange jumpsuit kid. *Bryan.* I scrubbed the soles of my feet, up my calves, my fingers pausing between my thighs. *Bryan's lips.* I thought about his hands caressing my skin.

I closed my eyes and remembered what his hands had felt like on my hips as we went down the slope, the way his fingers had guided me. It was a miracle we hadn't crashed. Ugh, and then in the lodge. I'd slipped a hand against his stomach as we kissed, his hard abs sticking out even through the sweatshirt. I'd been ready to pull him out to the Jeep and strip him down right then and there. The desire in his eyes…

I groaned out loud, throwing my loofah across the shower. I didn't understand how he could've gotten under my skin so easily. Sure, it'd been a long time since I'd had anyone in my life. Even then, Rick was more pusher and pimp than boyfriend. I rubbed the muscles in the back of my neck, working my fingers deep.

To my credit, it wasn't all sexual. When Bryan told me about his dad, it took everything I had not to climb into his lap and hug him. The pain was so plain on his face it was like seeing my own reflection. While it never gets easy, I've had a few more years to practice my 'I'm okay' face.

I switched off the shower and toweled down, squeezing the water from my hair. Not even a month and I was already falling for some guy I barely knew.

Every muscle in my body screamed when I rolled over the next morning. I got dressed, grabbed my yoga mat, and padded out in bare feet to the living room. It was only 8 a.m. but I knew everyone was already at work. Shifting the overstuffed foot stool and coffee table out of the way, I unrolled my mat with a crisp snap.

Rocking my head side to side, rolling my shoulders, flexing my feet, I slowly limbered up. I loved doing yoga first thing in the morning, the more groggy I was, the better. My mind remained calm, unfocused. I was free to move through the motions and gently wake up both mentally and physically. The serene world outside was a perfect view to look out on as I woke.

I stood at the end of my mat, toes spread. I took a deep breath, raising my hands to the sky. I bent at the waist, looked up, and folded in half. I jumped into plank position, surprised at how much my arms hurt from skiing. I guess I used my poles more than I thought. My back didn't feel ready for cobra pose, so I rocked back into downward facing dog. My mother blessed me with flexibility, so yoga was another thing that came naturally. Planting my heels on the ground, I pushed through my hands, arching my tail bone to the sky. After a few deep breaths, I released, jumping my feet back to my hands and standing.

It helps me, especially in the morning, to keep my eyes mostly closed through the sun salutations. As the energy in my body grows and I start to wake up, I'll begin to open them fully. This is why, on my third sun salutation just as I was easing into a deep down dog, I didn't see Noah walk up behind me. I had no warning. Out of nowhere, two firm hands grabbed my hips and a hard cock poked at my asshole through my thin yoga pants.

I screamed and jumped away, nearly falling over myself as I spun to see what was happening. Noah stood there with his pants pulled down to his thighs, hard, veined cock pointing straight out. He actually looked shocked that I'd reacted in such a way but made no move to cover himself.

"What the fuck are you doing?" I screeched.

"I thought you said we were friends again," he replied with a frown. He looked at me with dead, emotionless eyes.

It took me a minute to process that sentence. I probably looked like a fish gasping for water as I stared at him. "Friends don't surprise each other with butt sex in the middle of a yoga session! At least, not any friends of mine."

He reached down and grabbed himself, his fist encompassing the entire length of his cock. He actually gave himself a few strokes while saying, "I don't really mind where it goes as long as it's tight and wet." His eyes traveled the length of my body and for a moment, I felt afraid. We were alone and he obviously didn't like being told he couldn't have something.

I looked away, my expression filled with disgust. "Can you just get the fuck out?"

Noah frowned again, his hand dropping to cup his balls. I crawled backwards until I hit a chair and pushed myself up to my feet. Why was he just standing there like that? Was he so oblivious to my revulsion?

"I thought you said you wanted to be friends," he repeated slowly. His chin tilted slightly towards his chest, giving him a menacing look. "Everything I've heard about you, I figured you'd like it."

"Jesus, what? What you've heard about me?" I threw my hands up in the air, the back of my throat stinging with bile. "Fuck this." I was on the opposite side of the living room, so thankfully I was able to leave without going past him. My legs were so shaky. I ran to my bedroom, hoping I had enough of a lead that if he decided to follow, I could lock the door in time. The slammed door echoed through the open house. I clicked the lock shut and backed away from the door until my legs hit the bed.

I sat there for a few minutes trying to figure out what the fuck had just happened. I mean yeah, I've been grabbed before. Every girl who worked in one of Rick's strip clubs had horror stories of guys reaching up their skirts, but this was my house. This was different. I expected it when I was working, but this was my home, my safe zone. Noah's empty face hung in my mind's eye. Cold, distant, like he wasn't aware how bizarre his behavior was. And what had he heard about me? From who, Kayla?

When he knocked on my door a few minutes later, I was still so worked up, I screamed. Clapping my hands over my mouth, he knocked again. As he spoke, I scrambled to my side table and unplugged my phone.

"Liz, listen. I want to give you one more chance to make it up to me. I get how that might've been a little surprising, so I forgive your reaction. You looked so hot bending over like that, I couldn't stop myself."

I sneered at the door, my astonishment indescribable. He forgives me?

"Liz," he continued. "You know who I am. You know who my dad is. You don't want to make the wrong enemies in this town, do you? You only just got here. I like taking care of my friends as long as they take care of me. I can protect you."

"And I suppose that means you want me to suck you off or something?" I spat at the door. I grabbed a pillow and balled myself around it, pulling my knees high into my chest. My knuckles were white I was gripping my phone so tightly.

"I'd prefer a little back door action with that ass of yours, but I'd never turn down a hummer. Now, open up." My heart pounded in my chest and I couldn't shake the feeling that this was all a bad dream I needed to wake from. Noah slammed his fist against the door, startling me. "Open the door." His voice sounded artificially sweet, an edge cutting through.

I never let men intimidate me. Growing up with a

Marine for a father and in a testosterone-fueled town, I knew how to handle myself. Noah wasn't much bigger than me but it wasn't his size that scared me, it was his demeanor. Any other time, if a guy whipped out his dick like that, I would've just laughed him out of the room. Noah was different. "Please, go away." It came out little more than a whisper and I wasn't sure if he heard.

After a few pounding heartbeats, he hit the door with the palm of his hand. "Big fucking mistake. Huge mistake."

I waited to hear his footsteps echo down the hall before I called Kayla, my fingers trembling so badly I almost dropped my phone.

"Hey Lizzie, I can't really—"

"Noah just fucking assaulted me," I blurted. I was up on my feet, pacing around my room, the shock flowing freely.

"Wait, what? What did he do? Are you okay?"

"I'm fine," I said shakily. I quickly recounted what'd just happened. I'm not sure what I was expecting Kayla to do or say. Freak out? Call the cops? Rush home? What I didn't expect, was the laughter I heard from the other end of the phone.

"Is that all?" she giggled.

I stopped dead in my tracks. “Maybe I didn’t explain it well enough. It was fucking creepy. You should’ve seen his face and then he followed me back to my room.”

“So you didn’t do it?” she asked, the humor still in her voice.

“Of course not!” A thought occurred to me suddenly, the question coming out before it’d fully formed. “Wait, *that’s* why you’re fooling around with him?”

“Well…yeah. He *is* the owner’s son and it’s not like he’s ugly or anything.”

I felt sick to my stomach. It wasn’t the first time I knew of Kayla using sex to get ahead, but with Noah? Sure, he wasn’t ugly but there was something just so…vile about him. “And it doesn’t bother you that he just did that to me?”

She laughed again. “It’s not like we’re together or anything. We screw around, he puts a good word in for me. Seems like a good deal. To be fair, I’m not sure what you would’ve gotten from him. You don’t even work at the mountain or anything.”

“He said he’d protect me,” I replied numbly.

“Hmmm, that is weird. I dunno, hon! He’s a rich, entitled man-boy, you know the type.”

I couldn’t tell if the churning in my stomach was left

over from Noah or this was a new reaction to the mental image of Kayla fucking him. With everything I'd done in my life, it wasn't like I had room to judge but I still felt sick. "Yeah, I suppose. I guess things'll just be awkward in the house. Hopefully I can avoid him."

"Just put it out of your mind. We've got a party tonight and you've got that mountain man coming. Honestly, I don't know what you see in him."

I scoffed. "You're kidding, right? I got a good look at what Noah's working with and I'm not exactly jealous."

"Don't be such a size queen. Besides, it's what it's attached to that matters. What can the scruff ball offer you? Discount hunting licenses?"

"He's sweet," I said defensively.

"Sounds it. Drives drunk and likes to hit people. Real winner there. At least Rick never—"

"Rick never what?" I snapped. Even his name triggered my temper. "You and I both know there apparently wasn't any depth Rick wouldn't sink to. With everything that came out during the trial, I don't think I ever really knew who he was. At least Bryan's been up front with me." Kayla remained silent and I sighed, rubbing my eyes with my hand. "I'm sorry. I've had a really fucked up morning."

"It's alright, hon. I didn't mean to bring it up. If you like Bryan, I'm sure he's a decent guy," Kayla said softly. "I really gotta go. My boss is glaring at me through the door. I'm still editing that video from yesterday."

"Okay, I'll see you soon, right? We'll get ready together."

"You know it! I just have to pick up the kegs after work."

"Kegs? As in plural?"

I could hear the grin in her voice. "I told you this was gonna be epic."

"You can borrow something, I really don't mind. Just don't stretch out the chest," Kayla said with a pout.

"And how exactly am I supposed to do that? Suck my tits in? Unfortunately, the doctor didn't insert that feature along with the implants. I didn't think to bring any clothes like this," I said picking through her closet. Kayla was wearing a cute little strapless black dress with matching sequined black belt and stilettos. The headband she'd tucked into her hair had a little Santa hat attached, hanging at an angle. I looked like a slob in comparison.

I brushed at my patterned tights and sweater. "It's not like we're going clubbing. We're in our own house."

Kayla shrugged as she turned back to the mirror. "You aren't planning on losing your V-card to that douche bag, right?"

I rolled my eyes. My virginity was a constant joke to her. She'd been having sex since she was barely a teenager, the same time I was still dealing with my whole world falling apart. "I wasn't planning on it."

She carefully brushed mascara on her lashes, glancing at me through the reflection. "Good, cause you remember that's promised to someone else, right?"

My chest tightened. Shit, did she know? Did Rick tell her about the deal we'd made? My mouth fell open as I searched for the right words to explain myself. Could Kayla even begin to understand?

"To me silly," she giggled. "I want at that pussy first." I laughed nervously, quietly cringing at how close I'd gotten to spilling everything. She capped her mascara and turned around, looking me up and down. "But you're sure you want to wear that?"

"Oh whatever. It's too late to change now. People are already here." I picked at my nail polish and smirked. "I'll let you be the prettiest one at the party for once."

"You bitch!" she laughed, throwing a pillow at me. "I take it back. You'll be a perfect match for the scruff ball. I bet Noah wears a suit jacket tonight. He seems the type, doesn't he?" As she spoke, she lined the edge of her mouth with a red pencil.

I pulled my heels up on the edge of the bed, recalling the conversation we'd had in the kitchen the night before. "Are you really gonna take anything tonight? I'm not sure I'd trust anything Noah would give me. Jacket or not, he seems more the type that'd drop a roofie in your drink."

Kayla dropped the pencil and searched through her makeup bag, pulling out a bright red tube of lipstick. “Why would he drug me when he knows he can get it willingly?”

“Because maybe he’ll find it more fun without your consent.” I remembered the look in his eyes and shivered. The guy was a snake, through and through. I’m sure he was full of idle threats, but I couldn’t stop thinking about the last thing he’d said. What did he mean he could keep me safe? Safe from what?

She came over and sat facing me on the bed, dabbing at her bright red lips with a tissue. “He really freaked you out, didn’t he?”

I never enjoyed admitting to any weakness, which made my reaction to Noah that much worse. I *hated* that he’d gotten to me like that. I’d spent most of the morning hiding away in my room, leaving only when I heard the front door slam shut. I was so thankful when the decorators showed up after lunch. At least with them in the house, it didn’t feel like the house had eyes. “To be fair, I’m probably giving him more credit than he deserves. He’s just an asshole.”

Kayla placed a comforting hand on my thigh. “He’s definitely that. Don’t worry about tonight. I promise I’ll be safe, okay? Don’t feel like you have to babysit me. And I’ll keep Noah out of your hair."

I was still dubious but felt a small weight lift from my shoulders. Even if she was using him, at least it sounded like she knew what she was dealing with. It'd taken me about twenty minutes to get ready compared to her hour, but we were finally done and ready to join the party.

People filtered in by the minute. Everything was decked out in Christmas decorations. There must've been hundreds of feet of twinkling lights wrapped around every beam and banister. I wandered through the house full of strangers and spotted Morgan out on the deck. She turned and smiled at me as I pushed the doors open. Two long braids fell over each shoulder, her head covered in a multi-colored knit hat.

"Hey you, you ready for your first Powder Mountain party? It's gonna be crazy tonight."

"Don't you mean Angel Vista or whatever?"

"Oh yeah! I forgot. Better not say that around Noah or he'll flip. Different name, same crazy." She took a long drag off the joint she held in her right hand. Holding her breath, she continued, "A rose by any other name, right?" As she exhaled, the thick white cloud floating into the darkness above, she offered it to me.

Between my date with Bryan and Noah's wacko behavior, I needed to chill out a little bit. I grabbed the joint with a nod, breathing in deeply.

Morgan gestured to the DJ setting up on the far end of the deck. "In all the years I've been coming here, I don't think there's ever been a party with anything other than a tired old playlist on someone's iPod. He apparently came all the way from Denver. Noah flew him out last night."

I started coughing as I exhaled. "That's insane. I knew he was rich but I didn't realize he had enough money to do that. How many years have you been skiing out here then?"

"Oh man, you had to ask," she laughed. Morgan leaned against the railing and looked up thoughtfully. "This is probably my fourth or fifth season."

"Whoa, seriously? You look so young."

She took another hit and held it. "I am. I get that a lot," she exhaled with a half-laugh. "I ran away from home when I was fifteen, been living on my own ever since. I guess I'm an old soul."

"There you are!" a voice called out. We both turned to see Spencer walking towards us with two drinks in his hands. "I didn't know what you wanted, so I grabbed you a beer," he said to Morgan. Whenever she was around, he only had eyes for her. It was like everyone else ceased to exist.

"That's perfect, thanks." She offered him a hit but he waved it away. Judging from the panicked look on his face, he hadn't spent much time around drugs. I excused myself quickly, knowing that in no time Spencer would be edging me out of the conversation anyway.

I wandered through the party with my camera, snapping photos here and there. Not that I have social anxiety or anything, but big parties were never really my thing. The music was always a little too loud, people were too drunk. By 10 p.m. it'd become nearly impossible to navigate through the cabin without having to side step around groups of people. Every person under the age of 30 from Tellure Hollow was crammed into our house. I'd run back to my room to touch up my makeup one last time. Bryan hadn't said when he was going to arrive, so my nerves were on edge just waiting for him. I grabbed my camera and locked the bedroom door behind me. The last thing I wanted was the party spilling into my room and subsequently all over my sheets.

Looping the strap over my neck, I went straight to the deck. The DJ had kicked off and the music from the massive speakers reverberated through my chest. I crouched level with the railing, adjusted the focus, and took a couple shots of the Christmas lights fading into the distance. I snapped a few more photos of the crowd, group shots with the shutter held open so their movements blurred. The DJ spotted me and waved me over, pulling the ear of his headphones off as I approached.

"If you take a couple snaps and tag me on Facebook, that'd be sweet," he yelled over the music. I smiled and gave him a thumbs up. After scanning the area for a second, I grabbed a milk crate and set it up behind him. Standing on top of it, I pointed the camera straight down as he worked the mixing board and turntables. I took another series just over his shoulder and then closeups of his hands. I was getting so into taking pictures, I'd forgotten I was actually one of the people throwing the party. It wasn't until Bryan texted me that I remembered I was supposed to be nervous.

Hey, I'm walking up the driveway. I'm never going to be able to find you.

I switched off my camera and replied, nibbling the lipstick off my bottom lip.

I'll meet you at the front door.

I instantly regretted the sweater as I returned inside. A prickly sweat popped up in the heat, made worse by rubbing against people as I tried to cut through. I passed Kayla on the way and gave her shoulders a squeeze, overhearing a bit of her conversation. She was talking with a tall, pasty white guy with long dreadlocks.

"So, like, where are you from?" he asked.

"Santa Barbara," Kayla replied, touching my hand as I tried to squeeze past.

"No, but like, where are you *really* from?"

She groaned and turned away without answering, grabbing me and trailing through the crowd. "Fucking Asian fetishists. I bet he couldn't even find Korea on a map. Where are you going?"

I glanced back, knowing she wasn't going to like the answer. "Bryan's here."

"Ah, well have fun with that," she said releasing my hand and pivoting in another direction.

By the time I made it to the front door, I was a flushed, sticky mess. I spotted him immediately, standing in the doorway, scanning the crowd. He was wearing dark washed jeans and a tight long-sleeved shirt. My heart skipped a beat when our eyes met. Holy shit, the way his face lit up when he saw me…

“Hey,” I said breathlessly.

“Hey.” He looked down at me, hesitated for a moment, and then kissed my cheek. I cringed internally, hoping my face wasn’t as clammy as the rest of me was.

“Follow me,” I said grabbing his arm. I led him through the crowd, down the hallway, and to my bedroom. “At least we can hear each other in here. I just need to get changed.” I said as I shut the door.

I set my camera down on the bed. As I pulled off my sweater and dropped it on the floor, Bryan looked around my room. I felt a hundred times better in just a tank top. “I think you should know I’m not the kind of guy who puts out on a first date,” he said with a laugh.

I blushed a little, not having thought about how that must’ve looked just pulling him in like that. Thankfully, my face was already beet red from my hot sweater. “I know. A classy guy like you expects dinner first. I’ll buy you a nice, fat lobster next time.”

“Nice,” he laughed. “So uh, this place is incredible.”

I followed his eyes around the room and nodded. “I think I made the same face when I moved in.” I glided to the double doors that opened out onto the deck, letting some cool air in along with the thumping bass from the DJ. When I turned around, Bryan was at my dresser holding the framed photo of my mom. I padded towards him, the lush rug dampening the sound of my steps.

"Is this…?"

I smiled as I looked at the photo in his hand. "That's her. I think they were up in Vermont or New York somewhere."

"You look like her," he said turning to me. I took the photo from him, briefly running my fingers across the glass before setting it back on the dresser. My arm brushed his and I realized at that moment how close we were standing together. I slid my hand along where it lingered for a few moments, the connection like a magnetic pull. His mouth opened slightly as our eyes met, my desire to taste those lips all-encompassing. *Too soon, gotta make him work a little for it,* I thought letting my hand drop. "I think we should head back to the party." My voice came out a little too husky.

As I slipped on a thinner long-sleeved shirt, Bryan took a moment to look around my room. "I'm not even going to ask how much you guys have to pay to stay here," he said in awe.

"Wait! You've gotta check this out." I flicked the light

on in the bathroom, walking in a bit so I could watch his reaction.

Bryan's eyes went wide as he scanned the windowed shower stall. He looked at me with a mixture of shock and appreciation. "You use this?" I nodded, as if showering in front of floor-to-ceiling windows was perfectly normal. A smirk spread across his face. "Really…"

"Oh, you big perv. It steams up pretty quick," I said slapping his arm. I flicked the light off before I did something crazy, like invite him to take his clothes off and try it out with me.

I led him back out to the hall, making sure to lock the door behind me again. As I tucked the key in my pocket, I wondered for a moment if he thought he'd be spending the night. My stomach flooded with butterflies. I hadn't actually fooled around with a guy since Rick and even then…that was more of a business arrangement. After seeing Bryan laying on the sofa without his shirt, I'd found it difficult to ignore those urges. Even though I'd done pretty much everything *but* sex, I thought maybe he might be the one to show me.

"So, uh…why don't we get a drink? I think Noah bought enough booze to stock an entire liquor store and

Kayla brought in four different kegs." His hand slid down my arm, interlacing his fingers with mine. The sensation sent a wave of goosebumps across my body.

"Lead the way," he smiled. I wanted to lead the way back to my room and into my bed, but I resisted the temptation. I pulled him into the crowd.

I'm not sure how it was possible, but it seemed like there were even more people crammed into the house. A couple girls stood on the marble counters in the kitchen dancing like go-go girls. The kitchen island had turned into a beer pong game with dozens of cups on either side. The mood of the party was shifting as people became more drunk.

After grabbing a couple beers from the closest keg, we ducked outside and walked along the back side of the deck. Bryan still held my hand but there was an awkwardness between us. We'd connected so easily when he talked in the lodge. Maybe we just needed to be drunk or pissed off with each other to get the conversation flowing. I took a huge gulp of my beer and looked around, my eyes locking on an unbelievable scene. I tugged at his arm.

"What the fuck are they doing?" I gaped. I really, *really* didn't want to deal with someone dying.

I pointed to a small crowd standing around a mound of snow they'd piled up on the deck. Two guys were holding another upright as he balanced on the edge. He had a cheap plastic snowboard strapped to his sneakers. I rushed forward to look over the edge, knowing the drop was easily twenty feet or more. Down below was another group of guys with shovels, piling all the fresh snow into a makeshift ramp. Bryan stood next to me, a broad, crazy smile spreading across his face as he watched the preparations.

"He's not seriously going to jump that, right?" I half pleaded with him.

"If those guys aren't riding down that roof," he said pointing above us, "and completely jumping the deck by the end of the night, I'll be shocked."

"So it's really true what they say about snowboarders then," I grumbled. I almost couldn't stand to watch it. The snowboarder gripped the shoulders of the other two as they all counted down.

"Five, four, three, two, one, jump!" I gasped as the guy leapt off the ledge, the plastic bindings coming loose the instant he was airborne. He tucked and tumbled onto the snowbank below, landing in a heap at the bottom. I let out a quivering breath when I saw him move.

"They're fucking crazy. Who would do that?" I wondered shaking my head. We stood and watched another make an attempt, this time landing the jump and riding nearly down to the pond opposite the private run. I couldn't stand to watch it any longer, so I lead Bryan away.

As we rounded the corner of the deck, we came upon a crazy scene of a different sort. At least ten people had piled into our hot tub, some in suits, many topless. I spotted Morgan of all people, balanced on the edge with her feet in the water. She was still wearing her knit hat, her long braids framing her bare pert breasts. Knowing wherever Morgan was, Spencer wasn't far behind, I scanned the crowd. There he was, the poor guy, just standing off the side looking like the most uncomfortable person in the world. I didn't feel too bad for him. Judging by the bulge in his pants, he was enjoying Morgan's free spirit as much as the others, even if he didn't know what to do about it.

Thankful Bryan didn't know who my roommates were, I pulled him past quickly. The DJ I'd photographed earlier was really getting into it now. The deck was bouncing slightly underfoot as the large crowd moved to the music. Visions of a horrific collapse flashed through my mind. As I turned to say something in his ear, he bent to speak in mine.

Our faces came so close, our noses nearly touched. His hazel eyes scanned my face, lingering on my lips before he leaned forward.

"Let's go someplace a little quieter," he said, his breath hot on my ear. I nodded in response, my breath coming out in a shudder.

Traveling back into the steamy hot living room, I spotted one lone overstuffed chair. I pulled him over but we stood awkwardly, not sure how to arrange ourselves. The frustration of our nerves finally getting the better of me, I grabbed him by the shoulders and gently pushed him into the seat. He landed with a laugh. I'd planned on sitting on the arm but he looked up at me with an arched eyebrow, and patted his lap. *What the fuck? Why not?* I settled gingerly in his lap, self-conscious, like most girls, that he could feel how heavy I was.

Bryan wrapped his arm around my waist and pulled me close. His other hand slipped behind my head and pulled my mouth towards his. His lips were hot and urgent against mine. I garbled something in surprise, easing into the kiss as his tongue slipped between my lips. For several heartbeats we connected and when I pulled away, I was left breathless.

I stared into his eyes, for once at a complete loss for

words. The faintest curl started at the corner of his mouth as he ran his thumb over my bottom lip. "I couldn't wait anymore. Ever since you kissed me yesterday, I haven't been able to stop thinking about feeling your lips again."

The reaction those words created was a surprise to even myself. If I'd had more than one beer, I would've blamed it on the alcohol but as it stood, the reaction was all me. I bit my lower lip, right where his thumb had just been caressing. Putting a hand on either arm of the chair, I pushed myself up and eased myself into a straddling position, facing him. It was his turn to be shocked.

I ran my fingers through his messy brown hair and smiled down. "In that case, I haven't been able to stop thinking about doing this." I kissed him again, so passionately his head pressed against the black leather behind. His hands grasped at my back, arching me against his body. It wasn't my direct intent, I swear, but I could feel his cock stir beneath me. I squeezed his hips with my knees but I forced myself to pull back before I got too carried away.

"So uh, now that we've gotten that out of our system," I said pushing myself back into a normal seated position but still across his lap. "I think we can carry on with the rest of the night." It was a bit of a lie. It hadn't released any sexual tension. It'd only turned up the heat that much more but at least I could talk to him without the distraction clouding everything. I ran a finger along his jawline, my nail catching his stubble. "You're not much of a mountain man anymore."

He smiled, scratching at his cheek self-consciously. "Yeah, well, I don't actually own a razor so it's the best I could do." *God, he's cute*, I thought.

The longer we talked, the more comfortable I felt with him. I'm not gonna say we were kindred spirits or anything like that, but that feeling I'd gotten from the conversation in the lodge returned. The party nearly disappeared around us as we talked and before long, any nerves I'd had faded completely. We had a similar history, our hearts had been broken in the same places. We were two damaged people connecting in the middle of a hedonistic paradise, seemingly amazed that the other was real. I'd seen the ache in his eyes when he'd brought up his dad and I wanted him to know I shared the same hurt. It's not like I could go from one of the hottest kisses I'd ever had to talking about dead relatives. This playful date was shaping up to be so much more. I felt a pull towards him that wasn't borne of just passion but something else entirely.

"So, how do I get to wear a fancy pair of skis like you? I doubt you're making that much in the shop," I asked, my fingers twizzling through his hair.

Bryan tilted his head and grinned, his thumb idly rubbing my knee. His eyebrow moved a fraction of an inch. "A few more lessons, followed by drinks in the lodge, and I think I could get my guy in the pro shop to hook you up."

"Ah, I see how it is. This is downright—" My thought was cut off by Kayla flinging herself into my lap, belly first. The red lipstick on her bottom lip was smeared half way down to her chin. The smell of booze rolled off her as she laughed.

"I've been looking for you everywhere!" she yelled. She slipped down and landed on the floor with a thump, her dress riding up around her waist.

"Oh man," I groaned helping her up. I tugged her tight dress back down, saying a little thanks that she'd decided to wear panties. "How much have you had to drink?"

Kayla giggled. "Not much." She leaned forward and started petting my hair, staring at it like it was the most beautiful thing she'd ever seen.

I rolled my eyes and grabbed her hand, trying to get her to focus on my eyes. I'd seen her like this before but I had to make sure. “Sweetie, did someone give you something?” She kept nodding, almost as if she’d gotten caught up in the beat of the music.

She pulled my hair. “It’s just like the shit from Ashville,” she whispered. My stomach sank. I glanced to Bryan who was still sitting in the chair, looking at us with a bit of amusement. He had no way of knowing what that meant but a very tangible sense of dread leached into my blood.

I put my hands on either side of her face, forcing her to look at me. “What do you mean it feels like Ashville?”

Kayla pushed against me, her face twisting and contorting like a child’s in fear. Suddenly, she was on the brink of tears. “It’s like Ashville. *Snoooowbaaaall.*”

“Is that what Noah gave you?” She nodded, her face still in my hands. “Are you okay? You’re just high?”

Bryan started to clue in, realizing that she wasn’t just drunk but on something potentially dangerous. He stood and touched my shoulder, concern filling his face. “Is she gonna be okay?”

“Hey mountain man,” she slurred, her mood shifting yet again. She stroked his stubble and cooed as if she were petting an animal. “You’ve got pretty eyes for a mountain man."

I groaned and slung my arm around her waist. "She seems pretty far gone. If she took what I think she took, then I probably need to stick with her for the next hour and ride it out. Do you think you could help me get her outside? The cold air might help." Bryan put his arm around from the other side, resting it on top of mine. I leaned forward and continued, "I'm really sorry about this. She promised me I wouldn't need to babysit tonight but…"

"Really, it's fine. We've all been there right?"

I gave him a nudge and a knowing smile. "Yeah, I seem to remember someone from not so long ago…"

Bryan

I recognized Kayla from the bar. Even in my drunken state from that night, I remember thinking she looked like a real party girl. As I realized the full extent of her intoxication, it seemed par for the course. The entire party was filled with people half naked, throwing up, making memories they'd never remember. That's what your 20's were for, it seemed. When I saw the concern on Liz's face, I knew something more was up.

We helped her outside, pushing through the crowd to get to the front of the house. I still couldn't believe how many people were stuffed inside the cabin. I still couldn't believe how big the fucking cabin was! I remember pulling into Tellure Hollow and looking up at the houses nestled into the mountain, almost in disgust. A few weeks into my loner trip of self-discovery, I found myself shoulder to shoulder with every person in town. Not only that, I was interested in a girl for the first time since Angela had left me. Shock of all shocks, she was into me too. Any question I'd had in my mind about that was erased when she threw herself on me.

Even the memory of it caused my dick to twitch. The way she'd jumped on me was so fucking hot. Liz constantly surprised me, challenged my perception of her. From the moment we met on the bridge to the way she'd tackled the mountain her first day out on the slopes, I knew this girl could keep me on my toes.

I helped guide Kayla to the railing where the crowd thinned out a bit. We sat her down on one of the built in benches, looking at each other like exhausted parents. The girl kept pawing at me and calling me a mountain man, presumably an inside joke between the two of them.

"She's completely fucked," Liz said to me.

"Do you know what she took? She said something about Ashville, right?"

Liz looked pained when I mentioned that, as if she'd hoped I hadn't heard. "We met in college, in Ashville. One of our…mutual friends…sold a combination of MDMA and ketamine. It was kind of his signature drug. Snowball." Her mouth twisted as if the words tasted sour.

"Fuck, that's like an animal tranquilizer, right?" I looked down at Kayla. She was tiny, probably not even a hundred pounds dripping wet and she was taking tranquilizers. "Do we need to get help?"

Liz shook her head. "No, she's gonna be fine. If anything nasty was gonna happen, it would've by now." She brushed a piece of hair out of her eyes, tucking it behind her ear. "It's probably a good thing we nabbed her in time. If she kept drinking, it could've gotten really bad…"

"You seem to know a lot about this," I joked. Taking care of a potential drug overdose was a real mood killer so I hoped humor might work. Unfortunately, Liz didn't respond how I'd expected.

"You have no fucking idea," she said cryptically, her eyes focused on Kayla.

"I seems I don't know much," I replied quickly. It came out with a bit more bite than I'd intended. She glanced up at me questioningly but looked over my shoulder.

"Shit."

I followed her eyes and my stomach sank. The asshole from the bar was walking towards us. My fist clenched when I saw the smug look on his face. I wondered what Liz might think if I hit him again? Would that ruin my chances of a second date?

"Well, here are the two lovebirds," he said. I didn't

like the way he was looking at Liz. He seemed like a man split in different parts, his face expressing one thing while his eyes described another. His words said one thing while his tone implied another. The realization put me on edge and in my eyes, it made him unpredictable. "Where have you two been hiding?"

Liz visibly tensed as he drew near, even going so far as to step back against the railing. She ignored his question. "Noah, what did you give her?"

He glanced at me and then down to where Kayla was sitting. She had her Santa hat headband in her hands, picking at the little white puffball on the end. "I haven't given her anything she hasn't asked for."

"Jesus, just tell me so I know what to tell the fucking EMTs if I have to call them." Her eyes were like ice. The protective hand she kept on Kayla told me something more had happened between these three.

He waved his hand in her face dismissively. "She'll be fine. I got it from my guy. He's solid." He crouched down in front of Kayla, taking her chin in his hand and lifting her face. Liz moved to push him away but he continued speaking. "No, this little one here knows exactly what she's doing." Kayla's eyes flickered open, looking at Noah's face but then beyond. Her expression lit up like a child being handed a huge ice cream cone. The mood swings she was going through were disturbing enough without this guy manipulating her.

"Rick!" she cooed, pointing over Noah's shoulder.

I looked up at Liz in confusion and practically watched the color drain from her face. I looked to where Kayla pointed and spotted a man a little older than us standing in the front doorway with the strangest smile. He was broad shouldered with short cropped black hair. His ears and nose told the story of a dozen fights. If Noah had made her tense, this guy made it seem like she wanted to crawl out of her skin.

Kayla slowly climbed to her feet and ran over to him on wobbly legs. She fell into his arms with a happy squeal. "Ricky's here! Liz look, it's Rick." He kissed her tenderly on the top of her head, his eyes fixed on Liz.

I definitely felt like the outsider in this reunion. I struggled to make sense of what was happening. What annoyed me most was Noah seemed to be in on it, the realization immediately raising my hackles. He stepped back as Rick approached. He still had Kayla in his arms but was walking slowly towards us. Liz gripped the railing behind and I wondered for a moment if she was going vault herself over it like the snowboarders from earlier.

"Look Liz, it's Rick,"

I felt frozen in place, not knowing if I should step in and protect her. Danger rolled off this guy in waves and as yet, he hadn't seemed to notice me. Maybe I could jump him before he got to her?

"What the fuck are you doing here?" Liz said through clenched teeth. "How did you get out? How the fuck did you find me?"

"Does it matter, Beth? I'm here now." Even with Kayla hanging off him like a child, he still moved with menace.

Liz shook her head. "I should've fucking known."

Liz reached out and took Kayla's hand, speaking to her in a soft voice. "Hey sweetie, why don't you come with me real quick? I've got something to show you, okay?" In her highly suggestible state, Kayla immediately forgot the pile of muscle named Rick and blinked at her.

"Oh yeah? That's awesome, let's go!"

When she finally looked at me, the fear was vivid in her expression. I might not have known exactly what was going on, but I knew that look wasn't good. I fell in behind as she pushed through the crowd back into the house. I chanced a glance over my shoulder and saw Noah and Rick shaking hands like they were old friends.

Liz shoved through without apology, knocking people to the side like her life depended on it. I did my best to keep up but was bounced back and forth a few times. Panic rose in my chest when I lost sight of her, but I knew from the general direction, she was heading back to her bedroom. When I got to the door, it was locked tight.

I knocked softly. “You need any help in there?”

“We’re okay, just give us a second, okay?” Liz called out. I heard her come closer, the doorknob twisting in my hand as she unlatched the door. She opened it a fraction and peeked at me through the gap. “I’m so sorry about this. I had no idea—” Her eyes went wide and I felt a hand slap my shoulder. Liz slammed the door as I spun, coming face to face with Rick for the first time.

“Hey buddy, how’s it going?” I tried to say casually. The guy had a couple inches and several dozen pounds of muscle on me. Skiing might be great for cardio and a muscled physique, but it doesn’t build too much strength. This guy looked like he’d been sculpted in the prison yard.

“Good, good. Mind letting me through?” he said trying

to push me to the side with one hand. I forced myself further in front, hating that I had to look up slightly to meet his eyes. Noah stood to the side with the smarmiest smile on his face, looking back and forth like it was a tennis match.

"Ah, see, I don't think Liz wants you in there, so…" I tried to sound non-plussed, keep the confrontation low key.

"I don't think you're in any position to tell me what Beth wants." His eyes darkened and he ran his tongue along the edge of his front teeth.

"Well, given that this is *Liz's* house and you're not really a welcome guest here—"

"Actually," Noah interrupted, "I own the fucking house. As far as I'm concerned, if these two are uncomfortable with you being here, I'll put you up in a room myself." He clapped Rick on the back. "Plus, you brought the sickest shit to the party, so you are in my good books anyway. Fuck man, I'm so happy I called you! You're definitely hired." Rick shot him a squinted look.

He'd backed me against the door, so when Liz whipped it open, I nearly tumbled into the bedroom. She pulled her jacket shut with one hand, latching onto my arm with the other. She stared Rick down before turning to me. I could see the fake confidence pinned to her face.

"Can you help me with her? I think I need to get out here for a bit." I glanced inside and saw Kayla splayed out on the bed, looking totally out of it.

"Anything you want," I nodded to her. "Can you get her up?"

"Yeah, probably. She weighs nothing."

I stood with my back to the room blocking the doorway. Rick and Noah were laughing to each other. "It's funny, must be the thin mountain air or something. She could take a lot more back home," Rick said with a chuckle.

"Oh, she can still take plenty," Noah replied grabbing his crotch. Rick glanced at him, not entirely approving of the comment. Noah wilted a little under his gaze. They had a definite bad guy, sidekick thing going on.

I heard the girls having a small argument behind me and I mentally urged them on. Both these guys seemed a bit unstable and I didn't trust my temper around them. Noah wasn't going to be an issue but Rick looked like he could handle himself. Liz tapped me on the shoulder and gestured for me to take Kayla's other side. She felt like a rag doll and was babbling quietly to herself.

For a moment, it seemed like he wasn't going to let us pass. He got into my face, doing his best to intimidate but at this point I was ready to stand up to anyone to keep these girls safe. He was so close I could smell the beer on his breath, but he let us through.

My heart thumped like crazy as we weaved back out the front door and down the slippery steps. Liz started to panic when she realized how many cars were parked behind their Jeep. The stress of the situation was obviously becoming too much for her.

“Fucking fuck, I can’t believe any of this shit. Why are there so many fucking people?”

I kept my voice low and calm. “I got here late and parked down way below. I doubt anyone is behind me if you want me to go grab it and come back up?”

She grabbed the arm that I had wrapped around Kayla, panic filling her eyes. “No, it’s fine. We’ll come with you.” She glanced over her shoulder when we reached the bottom step and sure as shit, there was Rick watching us leave. It was like having a sniper’s sight on the back of my head. I was thankful I’d parked far enough away he wouldn’t be able to see the make or color.

We trudged down the hill, slipping a little on the ice and reached my truck. I helped lift Kayla inside the cab, putting her between us. Her head rolled onto her shoulder, a soft snore escaping her lips. As I let the engine warm up, I glanced over at Liz. She had her hands pressed together at her mouth and was breathing into them, not for heat, but as if she were staving off a panic attack. All she needed was the brown paper bag.

I leaned forward and put a hand on her knee, making her jump. She looked at me, eyes wide in the glowing green interior lights. As much as I wanted an explanation for everything, I knew now wasn't the time. "Do you want to just drive around for a bit or maybe grab something to eat? It isn't too late, the diner might—"

"Can we go to your place?"

My stomach flipped at the thought of bringing a girl home, even if she had a passed out friend attached and was running from No Neck back there. "Yeah, absolutely." I yanked the car into gear and headed back into town. My mind was a jumble. Adrenaline still pumping from the confrontation, arousal piqued from Liz sitting in my lap, I chuckled to myself. It earned a sideways glance from Liz, who seemed to be calming down the further we drove from the cabin.

"Sorry, it's really nothing," I said meeting her eyes briefly before returning to the road. "It occurred to me that I came here to get a little peace and quiet. I didn't expect anything like this to happen in boring old Tellure Hollow."

"No shit." Her voice was quiet, barely above a whisper. I felt instantly guilty that I'd even laughed, especially before I knew the real story behind this guy. The rest of the short trip was silent.

It was almost embarrassing pulling up in front of my tiny little ranch house after coming from the massive cabin. If she thought anything, she didn't show it. We helped Kayla inside and put her on the sofa, covering her with a blanket.

"How long is she gonna be out like that?" I asked.

Liz was rifling through the cupboards in my kitchen, throwing a look over her shoulder. "Depends on how much she took, but she should be out for the rest of the night. She's probably gonna wake up with a fuck of a headache though." She slammed the cupboard shut and muttered, "Serves her right."

"Can I help you find something?" I offered with a smile, stepping into the kitchen.

She spun and glowered at me before checking herself. Taking a deep breath, I watched her slowly exhale before she spoke again. “I’m looking for something that’ll make my heart stop running a thousand beats a minute. Whiskey or vodka, preferably.”

I crossed the living room in a few steps, reached into the freezer, and pulled out a bottle of vodka. Liz audibly sighed with relief, grabbing two tumblers from the cupboard and setting them down on the island. I poured her two shots worth but she gestured for me to keep going. I finally stopped at the half-way mark with a laugh.

“How about we start with this and see how you feel?” I said handing her the glass. She closed her eyes and took a big sip. I watched her swallow the harsh liquid, my eyes following her slender neck down. I shook my head, setting the bottle on the counter. The girl had enough on her mind without me perving on her.

“You’re not drinking?” she said eying me over the rim of the glass.

“Not with the pain meds,” I smirked. “Learned that lesson once.” I stood at the end of the island and leaned on my elbows, facing her. I didn’t want to pry, but I was dying to know what the hell was going on.

Liz took another sip of the vodka and let out a shuddering breath. Her shoulders relaxed and I watched some of the tension drain from her body. “I need to figure out how the fuck he found me. If she told him…” She shook her head again, taking another sip. “She seemed pretty fucking happy to see him, didn’t she?” She posed the question without pulling her eyes from Kayla’s sleeping form.

“She seemed happy to see everything, to be honest. I suppose that’s what molly’s for.”

“Well, he got out and found me somehow…” She stared at the glass in her hand and after a moment, her expression dropped. She hadn’t been specific but I was pretty sure Rick hadn’t just left a day camp to come find her. The guy had convict written all over him.

She gave me a sideways glance, her eyes the darkest blue I’d ever seen. “I should probably clue you in, huh? I’m starting to hear how I sound and I’m definitely coming off as crazy.”

“Totally up to you,” I shrugged. “Crazy isn’t such a bad thing, but this *is* probably the weirdest first date I’ve ever been on.” I waited for a moment, debating whether or not I should say what I was thinking. “Even so, I’m having a great time with you.” Her face softened and I was relieved when I got the reaction I was hoping for. I was afraid charm might not break through whatever shit she was dealing with. I uncorked the bottle and topped up her glass. "Just so you know, you aren't coming off as crazy. I have no idea what that was, but you handled yourself really well."

I set the bottle down and shifted closer. She pushed herself up on the counter, tucking her hands under her knees. I stood within reach, trying to convey comfort with my body language but I'm sure I just came off as awkward. She didn't seem to know where to start so I finally prodded a little.

"He's an ex?"

She snorted. "You could say that." Liz glanced at me, as if debating how to continue. "Boss would probably be more accurate." She slammed the flat of her palm on the counter with a *smack.* "I should've known when she told me they were dealing again."

A lightbulb went off in my mind. "Ah, drugs?"

She rolled her eyes, taking another sip of the cold vodka. "She and Noah have been cornering the market here, apparently. And you know, I had a thought that Rick might have something to do with it but I brushed it aside." She seemed to be mostly talking to herself at this point. "I just ignored it. He's in prison, how could he possibly be connected with all this? I figured Kayla probably still had a connection with someone from Ashville…"

"And that's where you met Rick?" I guided. I needed to know who and what I was dealing with.

Her jaw clenched as I said his name. "The fucker hunted me like prey. Looking back, I'm pretty sure I wasn't the only one he was after. I was just the first one dumb enough to fall for his shit." She knocked back the rest of her vodka in one go. "I'll spare you the gritty details, but let's just say a lot of his business isn't exactly above the table."

"Yeah, I got that feeling looking at him."

Liz's laugh startled me. "Yeah? The guy runs underground MMA fights. Got the money to start a whole league from his winnings. Broken nose, cauliflower ears, and twenty knockouts to his name." She laughed, "He's gotten a bit pudgy in prison." The humor dropped from her face and she squeezed my hand. "But seriously, don't fuck with him. He'd kill without a thought."

The last sentence hung in the air like a dark cloud of smoke. When she spoke, her voice was low, almost like she didn't care if I heard it all. "He offered me a job waitressing in one of his strip clubs. Clothes on, nothing inappropriate. The money was good and he was actually really sweet, to start. I started to think of him as my boyfriend…" The bitterness in her voice was heartbreaking. "I didn't want to strip, but I knew he had other things going on. When I asked, he made it seem like he was doing *me* a favor."

She took a deep breath and looked over her shoulder to Kayla. "She was actually the one who introduced me to Rick. Soon, he had me waitressing and had her dealing on campus. One day, when I came home early from class, I caught her counting out her money on the desk. Jealous would've been an understatement. It made me hungry. I was making good cash, but holy shit, ya know? She had so many bills, she probably needed one of those cash counters banks use."

The idea of that prick manipulating these girls, and who knows how many others, made me sick to my stomach. It was almost as if Liz could see it on my face.

"Don't get me wrong, he used us. I didn't care because I was making more money than I'd ever had before. But, even at the rate I was going, I was never going to be able to—" Liz glanced up at me, catching herself from saying something she'd probably regret. "Well, it just wasn't enough."

I rested my hand on her lower thigh. "You aren't working with Kayla and Noah. You got out of it all, right?"

She snorted. "Barely. Rick got picked up trying to sell

to a middle school kid, the idiot. I was in the car with him, so I got nabbed for accessory. I didn't have any priors and I kind of threw him under the bus, so I was let off with probation. Rick wasn't so lucky." She ran her fingers through her hair with a tug. "He got over five years in jail and I saw it as my chance to break away. It was just too close a call to risk the rest of my life for, you know? You can always earn money but you can't buy your freedom. Well, unless you're Rick apparently."

"What did your dad do?"

She shook her head and chewed her lip. "He never found out, well, not yet. Thanks to the lovely court system, I ended up with the same parole officer as Rick. When this one invited me out here," she said thumbing over her shoulder to Kayla, "I had to report with him and let him know where I was heading. I'm pretty sure that's how he found me, assuming she wasn't stupid enough to tell Rick that is."

I stepped closer, resting both my hands on her knees.

"What do you think he wants? Do we need to call the cops to let them know he's here?"

Her eyes fluttered a bit, as if she were seeing me standing in front of her for the first time. "I'm gonna call Kyle, the probation officer, in the morning and find out what's going on. If he's broken out or something, then he's who should know first." She dropped her eyes to where my hands rested. "As for what he wants? Your guess is as good as mine."

"Would he hurt you?"

She shrugged. "I don't think so…" Before I had time to question what her reaction might be, I gathered her into my arms. Despite the brave face she was putting on, she looked so fragile. She tensed in my arms out of surprise, but I felt her ease into my embrace, her hands gripping my back tightly after a moment.

"I'm sorry this all happened tonight. I was so excited about our date," she mumbled into my shoulder. "I thought the worst thing I'd have to worry about would be Noah acting like an asshole."

I smoothed the hair on the back of her head, pulling back to kiss her on the cheek. My lips lingered on her skin, the scent of her perfume filling my senses. "So, you were excited about the date, huh?"

It was great to see the half-smile spreading across her face. "A little, I mean, I guess." She groaned, and rubbed her face with one hand. "How did my life get so fucked up?"

"Everybody has a past," I said. "You can't get this far

in life without a little baggage."

"Yeah, well, mine just got piled up on my front step tonight. Special fucking delivery." She rubbed my arms and smiled softly. "I'm actually really exhausted. Would you mind if I go to sleep?"

I shook my head and stepped back, letting her jump off the counter. "You can take my bed. No, seriously," I insisted as she began to protest. "I'm way too wired to go to bed anytime soon. I'll keep an eye on Kayla." I offered my hand and led her into the bedroom.

"Why are you so sweet?" she said drowsily.

"It's nothing, honestly."

I tossed piles of clothes from the bed onto the chair, unearthing my photo album. My brief hesitation caught her attention. "What's that?" she asked as she stepped closer.

How to answer that…I patted the cover, tucking it under my arm. "Just some of my own baggage." I managed a tight smile and kissed her softly on the cheek. "Bathroom is there. I'll be in the living room if you need anything, okay? I'll make sure you girls are safe tonight."

Liz flung her arms around my neck, pressing herself against me tightly. I awkwardly returned the hug with one arm, trying not to focus on the feeling of her breasts smashed against my chest. “Thank you,” she whispered.

I turned all but one light off in the living room, sliding down the far wall opposite the sofa. The only sound was the quiet ticking of the kitchen clock and Kayla’s light snore. Still clutching the photo album in my hands, I tried to make sense of the night.

Liz

"Are you sure you're okay to drive?" I asked for the tenth time. Kayla shooed my concerns away with a flick of her hand, navigating down the slippery drive a lot faster than I would've liked.

"You know as well as I do, anything I did last night can be cured with a strong cup of coffee." I didn't have the heart to tell her she certainly looked worse for wear. "Mountain man's coffee really set me straight."

I rolled my eyes and poked her thigh. "The guy fucking saved your ass last night. The least you could do is use his real name. Bryan. Bryan. Say it with me."

She shrugged, a smirk curling her lips. "Whatever. Bryan. And what exactly did he save me from? You know Rick wouldn't hurt us."

Regardless of whether or not Rick had showed up, a part of me was glad we hadn't stuck around for the rest of the party. Apparently naked hot tubbing, jumping off the deck, and all the other craziness I saw had been just the beginning. judging by the state the cabin was in when Bryan dropped us off, the place looked like a war zone. Broken bottles everywhere, the nice leather sofas were either torn or covered in who knows what. It even looked like someone had tried to set a fire in the kitchen sink and one of the porta-potties he'd rented was tipped over and leaking blue sludge all down the side of the hill.

Thankfully, all my stuff had escaped unscathed and I couldn't care less about Noah's cabin. Besides, he'd already called in a cleaning crew to take care of it. Bryan had been such a sweetheart, really, he'd been amazing the whole night. He insisted on walking us inside the house to make sure Rick wasn't waiting for us. It was sweet that he was genuinely concerned.

"You do, right? You know that?" Kayla's voice broke through my thoughts. I refocused my eyes from the window back to her.

"Know what?"

"That Rick wouldn't hurt you," she repeated slowly. I had to bite my tongue, not only because of her snarky tone, but because she should know better.

"Well, after talking to Kyle, I don't think Rick is out

here to reconnect and get the whole gang back together," I said tightly. I looked out the window, watching the snowy pines blur past at an alarming speed. The parole officer had actually sounded nervous when I'd called him. He refused to give me details, but simply told me to be careful. Like, what the hell, right? "I'm not really sure what he's capable of. A lot of stuff came out during the trial and—"

"You know a lot of that was bullshit." Kayla always defended him. Ever since he'd been put away, Rick had been a real matter of contention between the two of us. I never thought she defended him out of loyalty but more because he was the best meal-ticket she'd ever found. As far as she was concerned, he'd never treated us badly or abused us in any way as long as we made money. She didn't see what he'd done as psychological manipulation or abuse because she wanted to think she'd always been in control.

"So what do you want to get in town?" I asked, desperately hoping to change the subject.

Kayla sighed, familiar with my not-so-subtle tactics. "Can I ask just one more thing?" she said as she sped towards a pretty sharp turn.

"Can you slow down?" I replied, bracing myself against the dash and gripping the handle above my head.

"What did Kyle say when you called him?"

I gritted my teeth, not wanting to answer, wishing I could delete the question from the air. "He told me Rick's lawyer was able to reduce the sentence and he was let out on probation because none of his charges were violent in nature."

"There you go. If the courts said he could get out, then what are you complaining about?"

I blinked at her, wondering if she were deliberately trying to pick a fight or if she really were so unaware. "He's still on probation. He presumably got out, went looking for us, and paid Kyle to tell him where we are. On top of that, he's not supposed to leave the state, which means he paid Kyle to not turn him in. Not to mention you guys are in business again." I wasn't about to tell her what he'd actually said.

The reality of the situation seemed to hit her, but like any deluded person, she swiftly explained away any of her concerns. "I'm sure that's not what happened. Why would Rick risk going back to jail like that?"

"*I* had to tell Kyle that I was leaving the state and you think Rick doesn't—actually, nevermind. I'm done talking about this right now." I shifted in the bucket seat, crossing my arms over my chest. We would never agree when it came to Rick and I wasn't willing to lose our friendship over it. She could be so fucking stubborn about him though.

"So…what did you want to get in town?" I started in an overly perky voice.

Kayla didn't reply, her eyes straight ahead on the road. As glad as I was that she was practicing safe driving, I knew silence meant she wasn't saying something. And knowing Kayla, if she didn't get a chance to say it, she'd make me miserable the entire day.

"What?" I huffed.

"You could've gone to visit him," she replied meekly. Again, her tone was enough to set me off but the implication was the last straw.

I snapped. "Listen, you and Rick have your own relationship. I never asked about it, I don't need to know, but you can't keep guilting me over the fact I never saw him in jail. He wasn't my boyfriend, he wasn't anything to me towards the end." She flipped her dark hair over her shoulder and glanced at me. We'd had this fight a half-dozen times. I just prayed she didn't push it too far. I tempered my voice and continued, "I'd really, *really* like to stop talking about him, okay? I just want to have a nice day out with you and try to forget the whole goddamn thing. So, for the last fucking time, what do you want to get in town?"

At least this made her laugh. "I saw a pair of mittens and a matching hat in one of those stores on the main street."

I sighed dramatically, crossing my legs back to the center of the truck. "Well good, now we're getting somewhere."

"Can we eat first? I think the Gritty Cask does a lunch during the weeks." She pouted at me like it'd do her any good, but this time, it actually did. The girl's body had been put through enough in the last day. I'd feel better knowing she at least had a hot meal in her stomach. Kayla was prone to living off Diet Coke and coffee.

"Sure," I replied curtly.

"I'll get you a drink," she said in a sing-songy voice.

I sighed, smiling at her. "Alright, it's a deal." I glanced out the window as we passed the spot where I'd met Bryan, my mind already spinning a web of ulterior motives.

Lunch was great. Despite the drama, I think Rick's reappearance made us both a little nostalgic, although we both deftly danced around any stories involving him. Before the food had even arrived, we were doubled over in laughter. We'd been reminiscing about past parties we'd been to, the good and the bad. Kayla reminded me of a themed frat party from freshman year I vaguely recalled, for good reason it seemed.

"Holy shit, I do remember this now! It was a stoplight party or something, right?"

Kayla nodded, wiping a tear from her face. "And you were supposed to dress in either green, yellow, or red to show if you were looking to get laid."

"Yes! And I thought I was clever as hell and went dressed completely in red." Memories of the night floated to the surface, memories that should've stayed buried. I rubbed my forehead and cringed.

"You got so drunk. All I remember is you walking around, going up to every guy who would listen to you for more than a minute and saying, 'I'm red, motherfucker. That means you stop. Stop!' and then walking away." She leaned on the table, resting her forehead on her hand as she tried to catch her breath.

I could only shake my head. "That's actually a perfect example of how guys that age think. I started declaring myself unavailable to everyone because, like some trick of psychology, they all thought red meant to just try harder. Like they could turn me or something."

"Guys of any age. Oh! That actually reminds me. I owe you a drink," Kayla declared, hopping off her barstool. She strolled right over to a couple local looking guys sitting at the bar. Moments later, she had an arm slung over each of their shoulders. They all turned as she pointed in my direction, so I flashed a fake smile and a half-assed wave. Within five minutes, she was strutting back with two bottles of beer in her hand, leaving the guys scratching their heads. If I hadn't seen it happen a hundred times, I would've been surprised.

"You said you'd buy me a drink," I chuckled as I took the beer.

She waggled a finger at me. "No, I actually said I'd *get* you a drink. Get. And," she said clinking the tops together, "I delivered."

"What did you say to them?"

Kayla took a slug of the beer and shrugged. "Told 'em we were single, had a party coming up, house on the hill, yadda yadda. They're married anyways, not like we have to blow 'em or anything. Oh, and get this! One of them told me there was a big party last night where someone OD'd. Isn't that hilarious? I didn't even know that'd happened."

I didn't find it nearly as funny. Running my tongue along the inside of my teeth as I thought, I sighed. "Don't you ever feel bad about it all?

"Bad about what?" she said defensively. "Look at you getting all judgy."

"I don't know, all of it." I couldn't look her in the eye, so I focused on picking the label off the neck of my beer. "Drugs, conning, all of it. Someone could've died last night because of the party we threw. There was a literal bowl of pills on the counter."

"And they would've had the best time as they went," she giggled. When she saw I wasn't finding the humor in the situation, she switched tactics. "Listen, sometimes I feel a little guilty, sure. But it's life. It's nature. There are wolves and there are deer. We just happen to be the sleek, sexy wolves. I don't see the point in apologizing for doing what a wolf does."

"I guess…"

"Look," she said grabbing my hand, "I know Rick showing up has screwed with your head but—"

"I *really* don't want to talk about it," I replied insistently.

“Okay, okay. I just wanted to say, I know you’re out of it all and I respect that, like seriously. Whatever business I have going on with Noah, it doesn’t matter. Rick or no Rick, whatever. I don’t want anything to come between us, okay? You’re my best friend.”

I nodded, finally meeting her gaze. “Me too, sweetie. I haven’t said it enough, but it’s been really good being here with you. It’s been too long.”

“Totally,” she grinned.

By the time we left the bar and picked up her mittens, life was feeling pretty normal again. I'd originally thought about stopping in Freddy's to see if Bryan was working, but chickened out. Fate had another idea. Well, fate and Kayla's credit card. I was ready to keep on walking but like a kid at Christmas, Kayla practically pressed her nose against the shop window as we passed.

"Ohhh, check this place out. It has everything." I nodded, knowing at least one thing that was in there. "Do you think we have enough time on the meter for one more place?"

"I'm pretty sure the town doesn't even have meter readers, so yes," I laughed. "But I'm feeling pretty tired. I'll go sit in the car and ward off any tickets, okay? Take as long as you want." She was half way in the door before I finished my sentence. Kayla plus money was a dangerous combination.

I wandered back to the Jeep, only a few spaces down and across the street, imagining Bryan watching me from the window of the shop. That same excited, giddy feeling flickered in my chest. I'd originally thought about popping into the shop to surprise him, but decided to play it cool at the last minute. I didn't want to appear too eager and I was still exhausted from the night before. A little secret about me…I get terribly horny when I'm tired or stressed. Made studying for finals in college hell.

Climbing into the passenger seat, I switched on the heat and leaned back, closing my eyes. I imagined him on the sofa back at the cabin, shirtless, his arms flung over his head. His eyes would flicker to mine, green and burning with the same intensity I'd seen at the bar that first night. He'd look me over quickly, his eyes scanning my body with a slight smile, before reaching a hand out. Scrunching further into the car seat, my skin tingled as I imagined him pulling me on top. The heat of his skin, his firm muscles, ugh…the way he kissed me like I was essential for living.

He'd slide his hands along my back, waiting for just the right moment and then in a swift movement, flip me under him. The sweet weight of his body, the cool leather on my back, his hot mouth on my neck. I'd spread my legs wide to give his hips room, hooking my ankles around his waist. I pushed my head back against the car seat, nearly smelling his scent, almost feeling his neck as I nuzzled in.

Suddenly, my fantasy shattered to pieces. Back in the

real world, my eyes flew open as Kayla knocked on the window.

"Can you help me?" she gestured with gloved hands.

My heart pounding from fright, I chuckled a little to myself. My daydream had become so vivid, my panties were soaked. I glanced across the street, wishing Bryan had carried everything over.

I helped Kayla load her brand new equipment back to the Jeep, piling it in the back with the rest of her shopping bags. The flowery skis and matching white boots certainly completed Kayla's snow bunny outfit.

"You definitely scratched that itch, didn't ya?" I said shutting the back.

"I'm just supporting local businesses," she laughed.

"So good of you." I climbed into the warm seat and clicked my seatbelt into place.

The sun had already fallen behind the mountain range, the town bathed in a deepening shadow. Kayla jumped into the drivers seat and backed out of the parking spot, her arm slung over my head rest to look behind. "Your mountain man was in there," she said with a unreadable expression, almost like it was an afterthought.

"Oh yeah?" I stared at the door of Freddy's as we

passed, my fantasy still fresh in my mind. Screw eager…there was something enticing about the guy I still hadn't been able to put my finger on. As we drove to the end of the street, I made up my mind to figure it out. "I'm calling him."

"Who's stopping you?" I ignored Kayla's snarky response, the excitement coursing through me. The phone rang a couple times, each ring spiking my nerves even higher.

"Hello?"

"Hey you." I cringed at how perky I sounded. "Kayla told me you were in the shop, so I thought I'd catch you."

"Ah, did she? She barely acknowledged my existence when she was in here." *He sounds so weird,* I thought glancing at Kayla. *Did she say something?*

I nervously laughed. "Well, I'm really calling for two things. One, to thank you again, from the both of us. It was really cool what you did last night."

He breathed into the phone, grunting a little as he stood, the sound of an old wooden chair scraping against the floor in the background. "It's really no big deal. I'm just glad you're safe."

"Well, it wasn't much of a first date though, I feel bad

about that."

"And is that the second reason you're calling?"

I smiled at the flirtation in his voice. "Maybe. I was thinking you could come up? I'll cook you dinner, we could chill in the hot tub…" Kayla groaned and started making retching sounds. I smacked her leg and shifted the phone to my left ear, staring out the window as we drove. "Whatever you want, really."

"How about I cook you dinner at my place? I can pick you up and drive you home. I guarantee no crazy ex's will show up."

"Ohhh," I laughed, "nice dig. Fair enough. Alright, can you cook? 'Cause I was actually going to make you something—"

"What the fuck is this guy doing," Kayla said. The alarm in her voice stopped me cold. Bright lights flooded the interior of the car. I caught a glimpse of her staring in the rear view mirror before the Jeep started skidding. "Holy shit, hang on."

I braced myself against the dash, turning in my seat to see a large truck driving within inches of our bumper. He flashed his high beams on and off while honking his horn. Kayla recovered from the skid, thankfully correcting just the right amount so we didn't fishtail down the embankment. "What the fuck does he want? Maybe there's something wrong with the car?"

"Do you think we should pull over or something?" she asked, her eyes wide with concern.

"What's going on?" Bryan's voice was deep and urgent in my voice.

"I'm not sure. Some guy in a big truck is fucking with us, driving really close, hang on." I moved the receiver from my mouth. "Kay, there's the gas station, pull over so he can pass."

"You okay?" Bryan asked.

"Yeah, I think so. We're stopping and at least there are other people there," I replied, then spoke to Kayla. "Did you cut him off or something?"

"No! He came out of nowhere."

I turned in my seat, squinting into the bright lights behind us. I couldn't see a thing but every cell in my body screamed *Rick*. "Why is he so fucking close?" Kayla moaned, eyes flicking to the mirror every second or so.

Gravel crunched under the Jeep's tires. She pulled the car away from the fuel station into the larger area of the lot, the truck still on our tail. As we came to a stop, she moved to put the car into park. I quickly stayed her hand. "Just wait. Let's see what's going on first."

For several long, agonizing moments nothing happened. The Jeep rumbled with the idling engine, the vents blowing hot air, but nothing happened. My heart thudded against my ribcage, every piece of me wanting to run but I was frozen in place. When will I learn to listen to my instincts?

"You're at the Texaco station, right?" Bryan asked.

"Yeah, the one just a couple minutes from the cabin."

"I'm coming, don't hang up."

"You really don't have to—"

We heard the door of the truck slam shut and both of us turned to see two shadowy figures approaching the driver's side. Kayla's delicate hand slipped to the console and locked the doors. A gloved fist rapped heavily on the window and we both jumped. Then, washed in the light from his truck, Rick's smiling face appeared at the window.

Kayla let out a relieved groan, which I wanted to slap her for. Even though she didn't have any reason to fear him, she left the doors locked and chose to roll down the window, slipping the car into park. I quickly dropped my phone to my leg but didn't hang up, hiding the glow against my jeans.

"You guys!" Kayla yelled. She was hanging out of the window, waving at the truck. Two figures walked in front of the lights, Rick and Noah. "You scared the shit out of me," Kayla exhaled.

Rick inserted himself into the open window, resting his arms just inside. His dark eyes were locked on me as he replied and I instantly got the feeling he'd been expecting me to be the one driving. I could almost see him recalculating. Noah hung back, watching the scene unfold like he'd orchestrated the entire thing.

"Sorry Sin," he said. "I didn't get your new number last night at the party."

My whole body tensed as he used her Rick-name, short for 'Assassin.' She'd been his primary dealer for nearly two years, her unassuming demeanor allowing her to slip into all sorts of untapped markets. Sororities, high schools, he'd point and she'd make a killing.

"God, yeah. I don't know what happened. I do remember being really glad to see you though," she said touching his arm. During their entire conversation, he'd yet to look at her, his eyes trained on mine. I glanced down long enough to see the time ticking away on the screen, indicating Bryan hadn't hung up.

Hoping my voice wouldn't shake, I spoke up loudly. "Rick, what do you want?"

His creepy smile widened, the corner of his mouth shifting with the curl of his lips. "Just to see my two favorite girls, is that a problem?"

"Of course it isn't, right Lizzy? She obviously freaked out last night but I think she was just surprised to see you." Kayla sounded like a child caught in the middle of a divorce, doing her best to keep mommy and daddy from fighting again.

"Surprised," he repeated flatly. "No, that's not the right word for it. I think guilty is more accurate. What do you think, Beth?"

Kayla laughed nervously, glancing at me, her eyes begging me to diffuse the tension she found herself caught in. Trusting my voice a bit more, I smiled sweetly at him. "Rick, I don't know what you're talking about. Why don't we go into the gas station and get a couple things? Then we can head up the hill to the cabin and talk." I prayed that Bryan was able to hear everything.

He squinted at me. Rick wasn't an idiot. He could smell the insincerity a mile away, but he wasn't sure what my angle was. If there was anything he'd stressed in our time together, both professionally and romantically, was he held honesty above all else. I remember him driving the point home a few months after I started working at the club. He beat one of the strippers so badly she needed her her left eye socket rebuilt, all because she'd been keeping some of her tips hidden before he got his cut.

Rick bit the middle finger of his glove and pulled it off, white teeth flashing in the light. He ran his thick fingers through his dark hair and sighed. "No, I think we're alright here for right now. Why don't you come out so we can talk properly, Beth? It's been a long time since we had a good…chat." The word dripped with insinuation.

I jumped as Noah tapped on my window. I'd been so focused on Rick, I hadn't notice him come around to my side. As he watched me with those cold, shark eyes, he tried my door. Locked. He motioned to Rick over the hood of the Jeep, telling him so.

I went on the defensive, fear lacing my blood with ice. There were only two things I had to do. Try and keep him as calm as possible and wait long enough for Bryan to come find us. I didn't think Rick would try anything in the middle of public, but his temper was unpredictable at best. "I talked to Kyle."

He snorted, his breath floating away in a white cloud. "Yeah? And?"

"He told me you got released, but I know you're here illegally." I spoke slowly, calmly, like you'd speak to someone standing on a ledge about to leap. "You're breaking parole by coming to see us."

A muscle in his jaw twitched in the light. "Aren't you the smart one? Seems you've gotten a real good education about the legal system this past year, haven't you?" He bared his teeth slightly, less smile and more primal show of dominance.

"You're risking worse jail time if you get caught," I replied. I tried to sound concerned and not terrified. The entire time we spoke, I kept doing fast calculations in my head. If Bryan left the moment he heard me say Rick's name, it'd take him a couple minutes to get to his truck. We'd been driving for at least five before he'd nearly run us off the road…

"Why don't you let him worry about that, sugar," Noah yelled through the glass.

Rick's eyes finally fell on Kayla, who'd shrunk into the seat. "Why don't you pop out of there darling? Beth and I have a few things we need to talk about." She rose at his words, but looked to me, hesitating.

I shook my head earnestly, hoping against all hope she could hear the threatening undertones of his words. She knew I'd given the prosecution information in exchange for a lesser sentence but seemed to think Rick wouldn't mind. If Rick beat the tar out of some stripper he barely knew for less than a hundred bucks, what was he going to do to me for ratting him out? "Please," I whispered.

Kayla's hands froze on the steering wheel, knuckles turning white with tension.

When Rick spoke next, all the pretense had fallen from his voice. "Sin, I can pull you out of this window with one hand if I wanted to. You aren't going to protect her from what happens next. You know what she did. You know there are consequences to our actions." I shivered as a coil of deep, instinctual fear wrapped itself around my spine. "So, why don't you just open the door and let me in?"

I screamed out as her hand slipped from the wheel to the door. "No!" In my fright, the phone dropped from my hand and fell to the footwell. Bryan's tinny shout was audible to everyone. Rick's eyes fell to the glowing phone, comprehension sliding across his face. His eyes went flat as he reached inside the car and manually unlocked the door.

Ripping it open, he reached in and grabbed Kayla by the jacket, throwing her to the hard ground like she was little more than a bag of garbage.

Noah cackled like a hyena, pounding on the window by my head. I was trapped. I briefly considered trying to fly out the back but one of them would catch me.

Rick slid into the driver's seat, shutting the door behind, and rolling the window back up. Kayla was to her feat but stood motionless, Noah quickly moving to her side in case she decided to intervene. "I think maybe we should go someplace to talk," he muttered. His voice was villainous, devoid of any emotion but dull anger. For the first time, I genuinely feared for my life. All of the terrible things he could do to me flashed through my mind, the worst of which was killing me and hiding my body someplace where I'd never be found. The thought of my dad going through that sort of torture absolutely wrecked me.

Rick pushed the car into drive with a violent shove, slamming on the gas so hard the tires sprayed gravel a few seconds before gaining traction. They tell you that your chances of survival during an abduction practically disappear if you let them take you away from the original scene. That's all I could think of. If I left Kayla, if I let Rick take me away from the gas station, I'd never come back.

I clawed at my seatbelt with one hand, the other grabbing the door handle. I didn't have time to think. As he whipped the Jeep around to head back into town, my door swung open and I rolled out. The ground rushed up to meet me, knocking the wind out of my lungs as I hit. I must've rolled three or four times, stopping on my stomach in a gasping heap. Even though I couldn't breathe, my only thought was to stand. *Stand*! Surely, he was going to reverse and try to run me over. He was going to come back and grab me. I had to stand.

I faintly heard Kayla screaming my name in the distance, my ears were ringing too badly to make out exactly what she was saying. In my panic, I figured she was shouting a warning. My nails dug into the frozen ground as I tried to push myself up and suddenly, a pair of strong hands were on my shoulders, yanking me upright. *Noah.*

I slapped against him, trying to free myself from his grasp. Regardless of what was going to happen, I refused to let him touch me ever again. "Are you okay? Are you hurt?" At first I didn't recognize him, but Bryan held me close to his chest as he shouted. I finally stopped fighting him long enough to shake my head.

"No, I think I'm…" I gasped, the air not fully retuning to my lungs. "I'm okay," I whispered. The panic rose quick in my chest. Where was Rick? I looked over Bryan's shoulder and saw his truck idling, door wide open. A few people standing around the gas station were watching the scene agape. Kayla stood about twenty yards away, her gloved hands clasped over her mouth. Noah had a hand on her shoulder, almost as if he were comforting her. I spotted the Jeep idling not far from where I'd rolled out, the memory so fresh it made me sick. From that angle, I couldn't tell if Rick was still behind the wheel. I doubled over, the cold air finally flowing into my chest.

"Where is he?" Bryan growled, his hand on my back. He was scanning the parking lot but with so many lit cars, it was difficult to make out which shapes were who.

"I don't know," I panted, "but Noah's still here. They were in the same—he could still be—" Just as I was about to say that he could still be in the Jeep, it's white reverse lights came on as it came flying towards us. Rick spun the car around wide enough we didn't feel threatened and pulled forward, edging up beside us with his arm casually hanging out of the window.

"Aw Beth, are you alright?" he asked with a smirk. His

eyes fell to my torn and bloodied jeans. "You know it's dangerous to jump out of moving vehicles, right?"

Bryan's hand tightened around my arm. "Go to Kayla," he whispered harshly. I looked up at him in fear. "I…I—"

"Go!" he snapped. I wobbled backwards a few steps, my body trembling in shock. I wanted to tell him to be careful, to remind him of all the things I'd told him about Rick the night before. The words jumbled in my throat. Kayla rushed up behind me, threading her arm through mine, but I couldn't pull my eyes away from Bryan. I noticed he had a rifle slung over his shoulder. That detail wasn't lost on Noah either as he came around to the side of the Jeep.

Bryan stepped between me and Rick, squaring his shoulders. The headlights threw bizarre shadows across the ground, dark figures stretched to impossible heights. Everything felt surreal, slow and fast at the same time, quiet and loud.

"Listen, this really has nothing to do with you. Beth and I go way back. I think you might've gotten the wrong impression last night," Rick started. He sounded like a guy trying to talk himself out of a speeding ticket but I saw his eyes dart to the gun a few times.

"Get the fuck out of their car, get back in the truck, and

drive back to whatever shit hole you crawled out of. Whatever Liz was to you, she's not anymore."

One of Rick's eyebrows shot up in amusement, the corner of his mouth curling to match. He ran his tongue along the front of his teeth, a habit I recognized. I'd seen him do the same thing when Candi insisted she'd given him all her tips.

"Listen, you yokel, absolutely none of this is your concern and frankly, I'm sick of you showing up where you aren't wanted," Noah said stepping forward. I got the distinct feeling that Noah had never been in a fight. Having Rick at his back somehow gave him the balls he lacked.

As Rick opened the door and stepped out, Bryan's hand slid up the strap, readying himself. I was so terrified I thought was I was going to collapse.

Bryan

"Lemme know if you need anything," Walt yelled out as the doorbell tinkled.

"I, uh…" Kayla's face popped out from behind an overflowing stack of hats. "I'm actually looking for a pair of skis."

That perked the old man up a little. He slowly climbed to his feet, grinding his knuckles into his back, stretching his spine backwards. "Well, lemme take a look at ya. You been skiing long then?" he said looking at her over the rims of his glasses.

"A little while. Do you have any skis with flowers on them? Cherry blossoms, preferably," she said in a cutesy voice.

I popped out around the corner, avoiding plain sight for long enough. "Well, I don't know what the hell a cherry blossom is but I'll show you what I've got." Their voices drifted away, muffled by the piles of jackets and gear. I scanned the rest of the workshop, hoping I'd catch a glimpse of Liz, but she was apparently back at the cabin.

I got straight to work as soon as Walt pulled Kayla away. The dirty look she shot me was apparently all the thanks I'd get for making sure she didn't asphyxiate in her sleep. I could tell Walt was in a great mood. Selling a couple hundred dollars worth of stuff seemed to perk him up to no end. It didn't hurt Kayla was a bubbly, young girl who flirted with anything with a pulse.

Grabbing the child's snowboard once again, I laid it flat on the work bench and sighed. The body was rippled and warped, apparently because the owner had left it leaning against a hot wood furnace. I did what I could, but a half hour later it was still a wreck. The bell above the door tinkled as Kayla left. "Walt, this thing is fucked but I need you to take a look at it. You might be able to work your magic."

He finished counting the money in the register for the second time, shutting the drawer. I'd nearly groaned when I saw she'd paid for everything in cash. *Gee, wonder where you got all that, honey...don't think the resort pays you that well.* I knew it was hypocritical to judge her and not Liz, but I couldn't help it. Something about her just rubbed me the wrong way, not least of which was her nickname for me. Walt tipped his head down to look at me over his glasses. "Magic, eh?"

"I don't know why you even said you'd take a look at it."

Walt ran a hand across the wavy board and nodded. "Ain't no magic can fix fucked. You're right. I'll give Grant a call later." He sat down on the wooden stool with a groan. As I moved to grab the next item that needed tuning, he exhaled slowly, blowing out his cheeks. I'd been with Walt long enough to know that meant I was in for a lecture. I snatched a pair of skis from the rack and checked the order sheet. Hot wax, great. It couldn't have been an edge sharpening or something that required loud machinery.

To be honest, I begrudgingly enjoyed Walt's lectures and rants. While he was nothing like my father, it felt good to have a father-like presence in my life again. I liked to think he saw me as a son, though his exterior would never melt enough to show it. My instincts about taking the job were spot on. For two years, I'd avoided everything and anything to do with skiing. Whether he knew it or not, Walt was a better psychologist than any of the half dozen I'd been sent to.

He sniffed and crossed his arms, watching me tighten the ski into the vice. “How’d the date go?”

I smirked and nodded, not meeting his eye. “Alright.” Switching the iron on, I grabbed the wax from the cupboard.

He scratched his chin idly, eyes still glued to the work I was doing. “You that bad in bed?”

I chuckled, dripping the wax along the ski. “Didn’t get far enough to disappoint her.” I glanced up, debating whether or not to continue. “Her ex showed up from out of town. He’s…uh, apparently in some trouble with the law.”

Walt nodded knowingly, like this sort of thing happened all the time in his world. “You take care of him?”

My fist tightened around the handle of the iron. I might’ve had a temper, but I wasn’t a violent man. All the things Liz had told me and all the things she’d said between the lines, well…it was enough to drive me to do some pretty terrible stuff to protect her. “I wasn’t aware of who he was until after I’d gotten her safe.”

“That’s good. A man shouldn’t be quick to anger,” he nodded. He cleared his throat. “If you ever need help, you can call.”

That sentence triggered a memory, my mind went back to something Noah had said at the party. At the time, I’d been so focused on protecting Liz the comment slipped right past me. "Noah said *he'd* called him…" I muttered, the scene playing out in my head. We'd been standing outside Liz's door, Noah jumping around like an excitable dog.

"What's that, son?"

I set down the iron and looked up at him, pressing my knuckles against the workbench. "You know the mountain owner's kid? The one I knocked out a couple weeks ago?"

"Little twat deserved it," Walt grumbled. He'd enjoyed hearing how I'd put it to one of the Richards. It'd earned me honorary townie status in his eyes.

"He was all excited because Liz's ex brought drugs to the party. Noah said he was glad he'd called *him*." I blinked rapidly, trying to make sense of it. "Liz thinks Rick followed her out here on his own, but what if the little shit had something to do with it?"

Walt scowled at me. "Why would he do that?"

For the life of me I didn't know. "He's a drug dealer, maybe that's why? Maybe he's looking to go into business with him? You said yourself the Richards family is pretty ruthless. Drugs have been flowing into the town for a couple months now, right?"

"If that's true, then it's odd your pretty little thing just so happens to live in the same cabin as that shit. And her ex just showed up, you said?"

The ball of tension knotted up in my stomach. The questions hit me in rapid succession. Liz couldn't still be involved with this stuff, could she? Was she playing me? Did she actually know who I was and therefore how much money I had? Why would she tell me all that stuff about him going to prison if she were trying to con me?

A wave of nausea washed over me as my eyes met Walt's. I'm sure he could see the fear there, but he had no way of knowing how deep it went. Could she really be that good an actress?

I jumped as my phone buzzed in my pocket. *Liz.* I almost didn't answer it, my mind already racing. It rang a few times before I finally picked up.

"Hello?"

The juxtaposition between Liz's voice and what I'd just been thinking was jarring. She sounded so happy, so perky. I couldn't believe she'd be capable of screwing me over but then again, if con-artists weren't good, they'd never be successful.

Walt gave me a knowing look as I stood. I walked to the back of the shop as we spoke, my worries thawing by the second. As distraught as she'd been with her ex appearing, a part of me wondered if she'd fall off the radar now he was in town. It seemed like she genuinely wanted to get together, so I offered to cook her dinner, thinking I could get to the bottom of everything.

"What the fuck is this guy doing?" I heard Kayla yell in the background. My heart jumped into my throat. I waited for the screech of tires, the sounds of shattering glass, the scream of twisting metal…and bodies. PTSD can be a real bitch sometimes. I squeezed my eyes shut but the sounds never came. Within seconds, my skin was coated in a thick sweat. I didn't remember moving back to the front of the shop, but found Walt looking at me with concern.

"What's going on?" I said with a choked voice.

I paced across the floor as Liz told me they were pulling over into the gas station. I strained to hear Kayla, to try and get a sense of what was going on.

"I'm coming, don't hang up."

"You really don't have to—" There was no further response. I heard muffled talking in the background, the sound of clothing rubbing against the receiver. I couldn't distinguish the words but I could hear the tension.

"Liz, are you there?" Walt stiffened in his seat. I paced

away from him, pressing my finger in my other ear so I could hear. There was a man's voice but I couldn't make it out. I couldn't make out what she said, but I definitely heard Kayla's voice. Then Liz spoke.

"Rick, what do you want?" An electric shock of fear shot through me. No one was that good of an actress. She sounded terrified, like she was hanging on by a thread.

I covered the phone with my hand and whispered harshly to Walt, jogging across the shop to grab my keys. "I gotta go. The fucker's there with her right now." Whether or not she was playing me, there was no way I was going to take the chance by risking her life. When Rick got in my face, I hadn't seen an ounce of kindness in his eyes.

Walt jumped to his feet, moving faster than I'd ever seen him, hands plunging into the dark cupboard beneath the register. He pulled out a hunting rifle with a rich, mahogany colored stock and held it out.

Holding the phone to my ear, panic growing strong in my veins, I resisted. "I can't take a fucking gun."

Walt practically threw it at me. "It's not loaded but it'll scare the fucker good." I tucked it under my arm and flew out of the store, thanking every deity I could think of that I'd decided to drive to work that day.

I put the phone on speaker and chucked it on the passenger seat, sliding the rifle tightly into the crease. The conversation was a bit clearer now, as if Liz had moved the phone to a better spot.

"Just hang on," I muttered. My mouth tasted bitter with fear. I had no idea what I was going to do once I got there. I just knew I didn't have much time before Rick took all the options away, maybe for good. "Hang on, Liz. I'm coming."

My truck screamed in protest as I slammed the gas to the floor, blowing through an empty four-way stop. If any of Tellure Hollow's tiny police force followed me for speeding, I'd lead them straight to Rick and welcome the ticket. It was only a couple minutes to the gas station when driving the speed limit, so I knew I could get there quickly. As long as I kept all four tires on the road…

"You're risking worse jail time if you get caught," I heard Liz say. It physically hurt to hear the fear in her voice. Rick was twice her size and didn't seem to be the type of guy who thought twice about hitting a woman. In fact, he seemed like the kind of guy who thought it was his place to slap a woman around a bit, teach her a lesson.

Rick's voice grew louder as he told Kayla to get out of the way. I cut over the double yellow lines as I took a sharp corner, seeing the glowing phone slide across the seat towards the door. My hand shot out to catch it and, of course, it was that moment my truck started to fishtail. I lifted my foot off the gas and the reduction in speed was enough to straighten everything out. *You can't help her if you die getting there,* I thought to myself.

Gripping the phone tightly in my hand, I held the steering wheel with my fingertips. It was my only lifeline to her for another mile.

Rick was speaking again but I couldn't hear it clearly, the sound of fabric rubbing against the microphone drowning it out. I only caught the last bit. "…what she did. You know there are consequences to our actions. So why don't you…" His voice became muffled again as my headlights swept up the hill. The gas station was only down the road.

Liz's scream echoed through the truck. "Liz!" I cried out. He'd gotten to her. What the fuck was he doing? I floored it as the road straightened, no longer caring about my own safety. "Liz, are you there? Fuck, Liz!" Her phone was still connected, the call time still ticking away, but the line was quiet.

Cursing under my breath, I finally spotted the glow of the Texaco station. I whipped in at full speed, the tires skidding on the gravel. I saw Kayla standing alone, her hands to her mouth in horror. Time slowed, the moments passing like freeze-framed pictures. I blinked and saw their Jeep speeding out of the lot, whipping around to head back into town. As the Jeep turned toward me, I could see the hulking figure of man in the driver's seat. Rick.

Something fell from the Jeep, rolling away in a cloud of dirt. For a moment, I thought it was a shopping bag or a tire falling from the trunk. As I slowed my truck to a stop, the headlights obliquely lighting the settling dust, I couldn't pull my eyes from it.

The pile moved, a delicate hand reaching out, fingers splayed in the dirt.

I was out of the truck and running to Liz before I knew what was happening, my heart in my throat. At least she was moving. At least she was alive. Now, I only had to get her safe.

With one swift movement, I pulled her to her feet. "Are you okay? Are you hurt?" I asked as she tried to break free from my grasp. I immediately saw the blood coming from a gash in her hair. I scanned her quickly, noting the torn jeans, the ripped coat. Swallowing the urge to comfort her, I embraced the other emotion thrumming through my veins;

anger. Squinting through the bright lights, I tried to spot him in the dark.

"Where is he?" My voice sounded foreign, distant. I held her by the arm, my eyes flitting to each movement, waiting for him to jump from the shadows. The white lights on the Jeep glowed in the dust, racing towards us. The bastard pulled forward and had the fucking nerve to smile at her.

"Aw Beth, are you alright?" Rick asked with a chuckle. It took every ounce of willpower to not rip him from the Jeep and beat him to a bloody pulp right there. I stepped between them, telling Liz to go to Kayla. Although I hadn't remembered grabbing it, it was then I felt the heft of the gun on my shoulder. Noah appeared from behind, a cocky smile glued to his face. He stood beside the Jeep, his arms crossed, entirely out of his element.

Rick looked me up and down, the smile on his face widening until it resembled a snarl. "Listen, this really has nothing to do with you. Beth and I go way back. I think you got the wrong impression last night." He was a cocky shit but the gun did give him pause. I'm sure if I didn't have it, he would've attacked me straight away.

I tilted my chin to my chest and gritted my teeth. "Get

the fuck out of their car, get back in the truck, and drive back to whatever shit hole you crawled out of. Whatever Liz was to you, she's not anymore."

The adrenaline was pumping hard and fast through my veins. It'd been so long since I'd tasted the sweet rush, the hyper-awareness, the overwhelming feeling of being alive. As Rick chuckled and opened the door, any fear I had slipped away. I was The Blizzard. I flung myself down mountains, broke records, laughed when others cringed back in fear. From the youngest age, I'd lived off adrenaline, forged in intensity. He might've surprised me last night, but I wasn't going to let it happen again.

Noah stepped forward, the movement pulling my eyes to him. "Listen, you yokel, absolutely none of this is your concern and frankly, I'm sick of you showing up where you aren't wanted."

He wasn't a threat. The real threat was exiting the truck. My hand slid up and down the leather strap on my right shoulder, reminding him of the gun's presence. With a laugh, Rick slammed the Jeep door and sauntered towards us like he didn't have a concern in the world. His eyes darted over my shoulder to where Liz stood and he licked his lips.

Rick held his hands out, exposing his palms as if he

had nothing to hide. “Hey man, I appreciate what you’re trying to do here, but these aren’t the sort of ladies that need protecting. These females…well, I wouldn’t turn my back on them, if I were you.”

I took a step forward, widening my stance. I knew with my bum leg it wouldn’t take a lot to bring me down, so I had to be ready to move quickly. “I’m giving you one last warning,” I said, my voice darkening.

Noah laughed, looking back to Rick for approval. “What an idiot!” Rick gave him a pat on the shoulder and chuckled along with him as they both advanced.

The fact they were laughing made the next moment even sweeter. Rick ran his left hand through his hair, his fake laugh muted in the falling snow. “*You’re* giving *me* one last warning?” He gestured wildly with his hand, probably meaning to distract me from what his right hand was planning. Keeping my eyes locked on his, I peripherally watched his right hand disappear into the pocket of his puffy jacket. The size of it, he could’ve been hiding a knife, a small gun, anything really. As he laughed, he stopped with only a few steps between us. Noah was completely unaware of the movement.

“Man, I’m giving *you* one last chance to get out of the

way. I promise I won't do anything to Beth she doesn't deserve. That should make you feel better." As if punctuating Rick's last sentence, Noah clapped his left hand down on my shoulder, his hand a vice-like grip.

A second later, Rick's right hand started to pull out of his jacket and I reacted. I yanked the strap down, grabbing the gun by the barrel. I brought the stock screaming towards Noah's face in a wide, looping arc. They'd had assumed the most dangerous part of the gun was the barrel, never considering it could be used in other ways. He didn't even have time to raise a hand to block the impact, the sickening sound reverberating up my arm. A bright spray of blood arced through the air, splattering on the snow at our feet. I readied myself for the back swing.

The sudden violence made Rick reconsider, his hand still hovering inside the pocket. Noah stumbled back, clutching the side of his face, red trickling between his fingers. He hunched over, touching his face gingerly, blood dripping to the ground with wet splats. Kayla and Liz screamed, along with a couple other bystanders who'd been caught in the middle. Kayla broke free and ran to his side shouting his name. He shoved her away, knocking her on her ass with a cry.

Liz was at my back. I wasn't sure if it was for protection or to hold me back. Either way, I was glad to have her trembling body pressed against mine and not his.

"Now you've done it!" Noah screamed. He was doubled over, blood flowing freely from his nose. "Rick, beat the shit out of him," he yelled, pointing at me.

Rick's eyes rose to mine as he slowly looked away from Noah. There was no fear there, perhaps a shred of surprise, but he definitely wasn't afraid of me. He made no move to leave but it was long time they were gone.

"I'll say it once more. Get it your truck and go. If I ever catch you around these girls again, I'll kill you." The words tumbled out of my mouth. To me, they were meaningless, what you said when you got into a fight like this, what characters say in the movies. If only I'd known the consequences of those words…

I heard a woman in the gas station screaming for someone to call the police. A couple young guys stepped closer, unsure who to defend should we come to blows again. It was obviously two against one but I didn't have a mark on me. After a few moments, Noah stood straight, looking down his broken nose at me. He leaned to the side and spit, Kayla gazing up at him in concern.

"Come on man, they aren't going anywhere. It's a small town," Rick said putting a hand on Noah's shoulder, pulling him backwards. It was obvious who had the real power in their relationship.

"See you around, *Beth*," he sneered with red stained teeth. Noah retreated to the passenger side of the truck. Rick took a few steps before he turned back.

"Oh, I didn't get a chance to say it last night baby, but happy birthday. It's a big one, right? Twenty-one…nearly a woman." The way he licked his lower lip made my skin crawl, but he didn't push it any further.

I didn't move until the taillights of his truck crested the hill, heading back into town. After that, my brain went into survival mode. I turned and grabbed Liz's elbow. "Get in my truck. We're going to your house to get your things and then we're going somewhere safe." She blinked at me, obviously not registering. "Liz, he's going to come back for you." With a tight nod, she made it clear she understood.

Kayla was just climbing to her feet when I reached her. "Liz is coming with me. We'll follow you back up to the cabin." She opened her mouth to speak but I walked away, dragging Liz behind.

I slid the rifle under the seat and climbed in. A few of

the bystanders looked concerned, as if they were considering stopping us from leaving. "Come on, come on," I muttered, urging Kayla to get the Jeep on the road. I glanced at Liz. She sat in the passenger seat staring at her trembling hands. My only thought was to get her completely safe. If I allowed myself to stop long enough, I was afraid I'd pull her close to me and never let go. We had to get safe and then assess the damage.

Touching her arm, I said, "You know what we're doing right?"

She blinked up at me, her blue eyes wide and heart-breakingly innocent. "We're getting my things and going someplace where Rick can't find me."

Pulling onto the road with one hand, I tried to give her a reassuring smile. "That's right. Think about what you need to pack now so we can get in and out, okay?" She nodded, staring blankly out the windshield. "Hey, we're okay."

"I know…thank you…I'm sorry…"

Trying to hide the concern from my face, I glanced at her a few times. She seemed shocked, which worried me. I could hardly blame her, but things would go a lot smoother if she were an active participant.

We made it to the cabin in record time. I backed the

truck in, planning for a quick getaway. Liz quickly jumped out and headed up the stairs. *Maybe I should bring the gun?* I chewed on the thought for a moment, watching Kayla run up behind. Loaded or not, I decided I felt safer with it. Slinging it back over my shoulder, I took the stairs two at a time, amazed at how little my body hurt.

I heard the shouting as I shut the front door. I cautiously checked the main areas before heading down the hall to Liz's room. There was no physical way Rick would've been able to make it up to the cabin ahead of us but that didn't mean he wasn't following. I wanted to be aware of my surroundings.

"What are you doing? Liz, fucking talk to me," Kayla shouted as I rounded the corner. Liz had a small suitcase open on the bed. She was quickly picking through her drawers and closet, moving swiftly around the room as Kayla stood in the middle yelling. "Lizzy! Will you stop?"

"We don't have time. We have to get out of here," she said flatly as she folded a thick sweatshirt into the suitcase. "Go pack, we're leaving."

"Hold up. You're bleeding. Will you at least let me look at it for you?" She stopped, scowled at Kayla and then looked over to me. It took me a minute to understand, but she was looking for my opinion.

I shook my head. “You’re alright. It’s already stopped bleeding.” Liz nodded and continued packing. Kayla threw a dirty look over her shoulder and approached her friend.

“Where do you think you’re going to go?” she said in a softer voice. “Christmas is in a few days.”

Liz didn’t meet her eyes. She spoke as she disappeared into the bathroom, returning with her toiletries wrapped in a towel. “I can’t think about that right now, Kay. All I know is the next time I see Rick, he’s not going to hesitate. We’re going someplace safe.”

I stepped forward, keeping my voice calm in an effort to diffuse the situation a touch. “My family has a hunting cabin not too far from here. It’s in the middle of nowhere. It’s safe. If you get your bags packed, we can go there straight away.”

Kayla huffed, throwing her hands in the air, ignoring me. “You just need to talk to him, that’s all!” I thought I heard the front door click shut so I stepped back, gripping the strap of the rifle just in case. The hallway was empty. When I turned back to the bedroom, Liz had closed the lid on her suitcase but was staring incredulously at her friend.

She blinked several times, speaking softly. “Just talk? I

just need to talk to him? Are you *fucking* kidding me right now?" Her voice grew louder as she stepped toward Kayla, towering over her not in stature but in presence. "You know exactly what he's going to do when he gets me alone. He's going to beat me. He's going to rape me. And if I'm lucky, I'll be able to walk away from the whole thing in one *fucking* piece. So please forgive me if I don't feel like sitting down and grabbing a *fucking* cup of coffee with the guy!" At this point, she was practically screaming in Kayla's face, who didn't move or respond. "Are you coming or not?"

Kayla sucked on her teeth and crossed her arms in protest.

"Ugh," Liz said with a disgusted shake of the head. She returned to her bed, zipping the suitcase up. "You have always defended him and I will never understand why." As she yanked the suitcase off the bed, our eyes met. There was an intensity there, scary yet admirable all at once. I took the suitcase from her and headed back outside. Pushing past the stunned Kayla, Liz followed me down the hall.

As we reached the front door, Kayla screamed from the bedroom. "You can't just run away with some fucking local! You don't even know him!"

Liz slammed the door and gave me a tight smile,

pulling on a new jacket. “Ready when you are.”

I’d been so shocked by her outburst, much of the urgency had sapped from my bones. I wanted to stop, clean the blood from her face, hold her close to my chest. As I looked into those crystal blue eyes, I saw the fear just below the surface, like bubbles under ice. “Alright, come on.”

The closer we drove into town, the more nervous I got. I half expected Rick to come screaming out of a side street, just laying in wait for us to drive by. Tellure Hollow was a small town. It wouldn't take long for him to find us and if not him, then maybe one of the police. As I drove past Freddy's on the way to my house, I thought to call Walt. Without a house phone, the best I could do was call the store and leave a message. I let him know everything was fine, we were safe, and that we were going to lay low for a couple days until things cooled down. Liz glanced at me with the last part, an expression I couldn't read in the dark.

We were in and out of my house in a matter of minutes. Like someone staring at the back of my head, it was like I could feel Rick just behind me. I stuffed a bunch of food into a couple shopping bags, grabbed some toiletries, and filled my backpack with a few changes of warm clothes. Even though I hadn't told her exactly where we were going, I was glad Liz had packed warmly. The cabin was never the best place to spend a winter.

As I zipped around the house, Liz stood hugging herself. We had barely spoken on the way down and I feared she was retreating into herself again. I jogged out to the truck and came back, scanning the house for any survival gear we might need. I remembered the extra flashlights I'd found in a drawer. I also threw a couple empty gas cans in the bed of the truck, mentally planning on stopping at the other station in town to fill up. I had no way of knowing if the cabin's generator had enough fuel and I didn't want to chance another trip into town.

"Alright, let's go." She nodded at me again, quietly following me out of the house and back into the truck.

It was nearly midnight by the time I pulled off the highway and onto the secondary road. I'd turned on the radio to drown out the deafening silence between us. It wasn't uncomfortable but we were both processing everything that had happened. What she'd screamed at the cabin as she was packing ran through my mind like it was on repeat. *If I'm lucky, I'll be able to walk away in one piece.* The idea of her even having that thought in her head tore me apart.

It'd been nearly a decade since I'd been to my grandfather's hunting cabin, but I knew the way on an almost instinctual level. When I pulled the truck onto the dirt road, I started to worry. The snow was coming down pretty heavy, the thick flakes flying toward the headlights hypnotically. I had to slow down to navigate through the accumulation. These dirt roads were some of the last ones to get plowed and it hadn't even occurred to me that the driveway to the cabin would be untouched.

The anxiety I'd felt in town slowly drained as I put more and more distance between us. However, it was quickly replaced with another kind of stress. When I'd first thought about coming to the mountains for the season, my mother had suggested staying at the old cabin. Even the thought had nearly triggered a panic attack. Nothing but memories of my father, of skiing, ice fishing, the entire life I'd had that was now cast in shadow. The ghosts of that life still lived at this cabin and here I was, driving straight for it, not sure if I was prepared to face it.

Ten minutes later, I spotted my granddad's mailbox. Hard to miss a big pink salmon the size of a small dog, even in the middle of a snow storm. Liz perked up as I slowed down, pointing the high beams up the untouched snow.

"Is this it?" she asked squinting into the darkness. Only the very edge of the cabin was visible.

"The only problem is, I can't remember exactly where the driveway is," I said studying the slope. Clicking the truck into 4WD, I steadily made my way up, hoping I avoided any deep ditches. A few tense moments later, the headlights skated across the front door, the ground leveling out. Breathing a sigh of relief, I pointed the headlights at the generator on the side. I felt more on edge now than when I was swinging a gun at someone's head. I concentrated on the tasks at hand, ignoring where I was for the time being.

As I filled the generator with one of the gas canisters, Liz got out of the truck and grabbed her suitcase from the back. "The door is probably unlocked if you wanna test it," I said glancing up.

"Seriously?"

"There's nothing inside worth stealing. The closest house is a couple miles in every direction. And my grandfather was a trusting man."

Liz scowled and then shrugged, testing the doorknob. The door swung open, the creak of it alone unleashing a flood of memories. I kicked myself. I'd been so intent on getting her to a safe place, I didn't stop to consider what it might do to me. The last time I'd been up here, Dad and I had gone hiking in the woods. *He'd just bought that new pack for me and I couldn't wait to test it out*...I pushed the memory away with a shake of my head. I finished pouring the gasoline into the tank and thankfully, the generator quickly stuttered to life.

Stepping past Liz in the doorway, I felt along the wall for the light switch I knew was there. A single overhead light flickered on, bathing the dusty cabin in a pale yellow light. I looked at her, an apology on my lips. What the hell was I thinking taking her up here? We should've gone to Denver or something, stayed in a hotel.

"Thank you," she whispered.

"I…uh…" I stared at her, completely at a loss for words. "I'll go get the rest of the stuff," I finally blurted. "Stay here."

After dragging everything else inside, I quickly assessed what we had, trying to ignore the memories each object held. The tiny stove was electric and seemed to work, unlike the fridge. We'd have to keep the perishable food outside in the snow, which was fine. The toilet worked, but smelled faintly like the septic tank when it was flushed. The water for the shower was heated on a tank up on the roof, gravity providing the water pressure. We'd have to wait till the afternoon if we wanted to use it. I also managed to unearth a single lamp, which was much better than the harsh overhead light.

Liz busied herself by taking the blankets off the sofa

and bed, sending clouds of dust into the air. I couldn't help but watch her out of the corner of my eye. What was she thinking? How was she actually handling all this?

Her lips curled into a small smile. "I'm not going to have a breakdown, if that's what you're wondering," she said without looking at me. "I'm just fucking freezing." She patted the pillows on the small double bed, covering her face in the crook of her arm to avoid the dust. *Dad was probably the last person to sleep on that bed,* I thought idly.

Again, pulling myself from the memory, I returned my attention to the furnace. I'd piled the wood just so, inserting a few strips of fat wood to make sure it caught the first time. The rolled newspaper caught and the dark iron furnace glowed with flickering orange light. I knelt in front of it, watching the embers snake along the print, changing color with the flame. I felt like I was being torn in three directions. The ghosts of the past in this place, the dangers of the present threatening us, and perhaps my future, watching me light the fire.

"Holy shit," I heard Liz shiver. She was curled into a tight ball on the old patterned sofa, rubbing her hands together. The blood on her forehead was dried and dark.

"Let's get you cleaned up," I said rocking to my feet. I

grabbed a cushion from the sofa and threw it on the ground in front of the fire. “Come sit here. I’m gonna take a look at your cuts.”

“I’m really fine,” she insisted. The look I gave her was enough to end any further arguments. She rolled her eyes, making out that I was being overbearing. “Alright, have it your way.”

Líz

The English language hasn't developed words to describe how I was feeling. As Bryan sat beside me wiping blood from my hair, all I could think of was what it'd be like to feel his hot skin against mine. I nearly reached out to touch his face, stopping just short. Maybe I was in shock, my addled brain turning to sex as a form of distraction, as if I wanted to be distracted by Bryan. They say your emotions run high during episodes of high stress. If my ex whatever-the-fuck-he-was coming back and nearly kidnapping me wasn't high stress, I'm not sure what is.

I trained my eyes on the growing flames as Bryan inspected the cut on my head. As a way to take my mind off wanting to jump him right then and there, I started talking. The words poured from my mouth like an open faucet. I guess a part of me wanted to find an explanation, either for myself or for him. With everything he'd done, I owed him that much…

"I lost my mom when I was little. She died of a particularly aggressive form of breast cancer. One of her sisters died from it and my other aunt is still fighting." My voice sounded foreign, devoid of emotion.

"God, that's terrible…" he said, his hand pausing on my head. I closed my eyes as Bryan brushed the hair out of my face, tucking it behind my ear. He dabbed the cut with a wet cloth and I continued.

"Yeah, well, seems the women in my family are predisposed to it. Mom didn't find out until she was Stage 4. It was already too late," my voice quivered at the end. He reached out for my hand, which I took but held limply. "Anyway, she died just as I was going through puberty, you know? It was terrible. I started developing these breasts that I knew were all but a death sentence for me. I just remember crying all the time, wanting to rip them off."

I felt like I was thirteen again, scared, lonely. I tried so hard to not think about her death, even though everything I did, the person I was, sprung from the event. I remembered he'd lost his dad as well, so I knew he could understand. In that regard, I felt connected to him but had to remember we were still essentially strangers.

"When I turned eighteen, I went into the hospital, had

them replaced with ones that were less likely to kill me," I said grabbing one of my breasts quickly, letting my hand fall back into my lap. Bryan frowned, his eyes filled with concern I could hardly stand to see.

"Aw man, and I was such an asshole the other night." I felt my face flush. He had been a dick, but I'd severely overreacted. "God, I'm so sorry."

I shrugged. "I'm still pretty sensitive about it. It's only been a couple years and it wasn't your fault, really."

Bryan took my hands in his, turning the palms upward. In the growing fire, I could see the scrapes, bits of gravel embedded in the skin. I looked up into his green eyes and sighed. "This is gonna hurt, isn't it?"

He winced at the idea. "I'll make it quick." He led me into the bathroom, pulling the coat from my shoulders. I sat on the closed toilet, watching him from the corner of my eye. When I'd gotten back to the house, I'd changed my coat but didn't think to change my clothes. When I rolled out of the Jeep to get away from Rick, I'd landed on my elbows and forearms, tearing through the thin fabric to my skin. The sleeves of my shirt were torn, stuck to my flesh with dark blood. "Shit Liz, are you sure you're alright? This is a pretty gnarly road rash."

I shook my head. Whether the numbness came from the cold or my emotions, it dulled any pain I should've been feeling.

He soaked a washcloth in cold water and pressed it to the fabric so it would pull away gently, not tear. I kept talking, staring off into space.

"So yeah, since the surgery was voluntary—actually they called it a 'prophylactic mastectomy'—we had to pay out of pocket for it."

"The government didn't help out? I thought you said your dad was in the Marines?"

I shook my head, kicking my feet out and pointing my toes together. "Not a cent. The procedure went well but then I got a fucking infection, so I ended up staying in the hospital for almost two weeks." My voice dropped to almost a whisper. I realized with a twist in my gut that it was the first time I'd ever run through the entire story. Framing it made everything so much…clearer. "My dad had to sell the house to even put a dent in the payments. I went back to work as soon as I could, but you don't save up a whole lot when you're working at Dairy Queen." I pressed my lips together and whispered, "It was their house, the one they'd bought together."

Bryan set the stained cloth down and examined my arms. He sighed and met my eyes. “You’re gonna have to take your shirt off so I can clean these properly.” The embarrassment in his voice made me smile.

“Already trying to get my clothes off, eh?” I said with a wink. Knowing my black shelf bra was wide enough to cover the scars under my breasts, I didn’t mind pulling the ruined shirt over my head. He grabbed a blanket from the other room and wrapped it around my naked shoulders, giving my arms a little rub before returning to the floor in front of me. I held my arm out, the skin raw and scraped. Luckily, it didn’t look like there were any deep gashes.

Despite the cold, the touch of his hands made my body tingle with warmth. I pressed my knees together and closed my eyes, trying to ignore the ridiculous arousal happening beyond my control. Instead, I spoke. “Dad insisted I go to school, even though I had no idea what I wanted to study. I picked a college that was close enough to home I could drive back ‘cause I hated the idea of leaving him all alone.

“It was only a few months after the surgery when I met Rick. I was terrified at first. He’s a mean looking guy, you know? But he was nice to me and Kayla vouched for him. We went out a couple times in a group, but he was…intense.

"One night, I got really drunk when we were out and this random guy was all over me. Rick scared him off and…I don't know. I guess I have a thing for knights in shining armor." Bryan's hand paused for a moment but quickly continued, my not-so-subtle message received. "He'd decided he wanted me and that was it. He knew I needed money…"

"And you started working at one of the clubs he owned, right?" It sounded so cliche when he said it. Girl with broken wing gets taken advantage of by big, bad wolf. That's my life, though. I decided the sooner I admitted it to myself, the sooner I could move past it, maybe with Bryan's help…assuming I didn't completely scare him away.

"I started with waitressing in the clubs and moved to dancing in one of the cages. I always wore a bikini or something, never naked, and some nights I earned more money than the girls who took it all off. It was good money, more than enough money, but I wanted more." I shook my head bitterly. "I saw him hit the girls I can't tell you how many times. He was a real asshole to them, but I was blind to it. Kayla loved him, he never raised a hand to me…"

"You were doing the best you could, I get it," Bryan said trying to comfort me. I appreciated the gesture, but he still didn't know the whole story.

"It was like I was leading two different lives. My dad thought I was doing well at school, making something of myself. He isn't real tech savvy, so I was able to forge my grades and keep him in the dark. To everyone else, everyone other than Kayla really, I was a slacker. I was the girl in the dorm they came to if they wanted to score some weed or coke or Rick's signature 'Snowball.'"

"One of Rick's runners got picked up by the cops once and I filled in. You know, in movies they always make drug deals seem so cagey and serious but it's not. It's just like a pizza delivery or something. They call up, I'd run it over. Simple. He gives all his runners a percentage of the sale, says it's more risk so they deserve a greater reward." I shook my head. They were all my own memories but it felt like I was talking about someone else. I was describing the things another Liz had done. No. I was describing things *Beth* had done…

Bryan dried off my arms and applied the bandages. My eyes shot open when he rested his hands on my thighs, the contact felt so intimate. "I know what you're gonna say, but your knees look pretty bad too." There was a sparkle in his eye, but his expression remained serious.

"Oh do they now?" I said, my hands dropping from the scratchy blanket around my shoulders to my pants. I quickly undid them, pulling them down in one swift movement. After a cursory inspection, I decided the tears and blood had ruined the jeans, so I balled them up and threw them in the corner with my bloodied shirt. Pulling the blanket tighter, I did my best to ignore the cold air on my skin.

"Actually, they aren't as bad as I thought..." he mumbled as he started to clean them.

I couldn't stand the thought of him seeing me as a bad person. I might've done bad things, but fucking hell, I *wasn't* a bad person! "I know it sounds awful, but you have to try and understand. Between the club and the drugs, I was pulling in thousands every week. Even with so much money coming in, it would've taken me years to earn enough to pay my dad back." I closed my eyes and tilted my head back, blinking the tears away. "The plan was that I'd graduate without any debt, medical or otherwise *and* have enough money to buy my parent's house back."

I rested my chin to my chest, feeling the weight of the entire situation come crashing down around me. My gaze fell to his hands as he smoothed the last bandage over my knee. The image rocked me. Here was I was, patched up, damaged.

Hot tears prickled the corners of my eyes and I knew I couldn't stop the flow. "If Rick is good at anything, it's knowing exactly what someone wants so he can twist it to his own advantage. He knew I needed the money. I never told him why, I never let him in that closely, but he could sense the desperation," my voice cracked. "That's why it didn't take him too long…to convince me…for me to accept that offer…" I couldn't continue. Reduced to sobs, I finally faced the darkest thing I'd ever done.

"Hey, whoa there." Bryan pressed into me, wrapping his arms tightly around my blanketed body. I was aware of being nearly naked but yearned for the comfort. I shifted my knees, wrapping my legs around his body as I opened up my arms. His cold hands slid against my bare skin but I didn't mind. For several minutes, he held me while I cried, the shadows of my past flying forward to confront me. Without a word, he slipped his hands under my ass and picked me up, carrying me into the other room. After gently setting me down on the squeaky bed, my tears began to slow.

"We need to get you dressed. Do you care what I pick out? I'm not the best with women's fashion." I shook my head, wiping my cheeks with the back of my hand. I watched as he plucked a small tank top, thick sweatshirt, and black tights from my suitcase. He helped me pull the clothes on over the bandages, making sure none of the tape stuck to the fabric. Once I was fully dressed, I stood trembling in his arms. Concern filled his eyes. "Come here, let's get you warm."

Bryan threw another log on the fire as I sat down on the cushion. I could tell it was definitely cutting through the cold. He settled behind me so I sat between his legs, wrapping the blanket around our shoulders, his arm slipping around my waist to hold me. Before long, my face was hot from the fire, the rest of me warmed by his body heat. I shifted slightly so I could rest my head on his chest, closing my eyes as I listened to the steady beat of his strong heart.

"I'm sorry."

"For what? You have nothing to be sorry for," he said smoothing my hair.

But I was sorry. For crying. For dragging him into this whole mess. For dumping my whole life story on one of the nicest guys I'd ever met. I looked up, his eyes glittering in the firelight. "I…I just…"

Our mouths slowly drew together, each of us unsure if it were okay to continue. I took a deep breath the moment our lips touched, the contact like an electric current running through my body. His right hand slid up the back of my neck, fingers delving into my hair. His tongue softly parted my lips, slipping between in search of mine. The way my body reacted left me breathless. Every inch of my skin zinged with the lightest contact, swirling together deep in my core until I practically pulsed with desire. What started as a soft kiss quickly built to something so much more. He sucked my lower lip into his mouth, my tongue danced with his.

I wanted to show him how glad I was to have him in my life, to show him physically when the words had failed me. I pulled away for only a moment, our eyes locked on one another. I shifted in his arms, spinning until I faced him, my bent knees on either side of his torso. Sliding my hands to the sides of his face, I brought my mouth down on his, a hard, lust-filled kiss.

Bryan's hand slipped beneath my sweatshirt, fingers digging into the flesh of my back. I clawed at the zipper on his dark hoodie, pulling it open and off his shoulders. My hands ran along the taught muscles of his chest. I remembered the scars I'd glimpsed back in the cabin, hiding beneath his shirt. He pulled my face back to his with a finger under my chin, gazing into my eyes before he devoured my mouth again. The heat in my core was white hot, my pussy slick with anticipation.

It was my turn to strip. He pulled the sweatshirt over my head, his hot mouth immediately on my exposed neck. I arched into him, his hands gathering me closer at the small of my back. A groan escaped my lips which seemed to drive him crazy. He tried to pull down the strap of my tank top but I froze up, shifting my arm around his neck so he couldn't. His hand slipped under the top, the contact causing a cascade of shivers to ripple through me.

He kissed my bottom lip, my chin, my jaw. I tilted my head back as he kissed down my throat to the edge of my collarbone. At the same time, his hand pushed up, tracing a path from my waist to my belly, searching for my breasts.

I wanted to let him touch me. God, I practically needed it for my own sanity. As much as I wanted to, I just couldn't show him my scars yet. After all the events of the day, that was my hard limit. A fraction away from the bottom of my breast, I slapped my hand against his, stopping suddenly. He furrowed his brow in confusion but immediately pulled his hand from under the top.

"I'm sorry, I didn't mean to push you," he said holding my face in his hand. "I'm so sorry. I didn't think. You're just so brave and beautiful…" His sincerity crumbled what little defenses I had left. I managed to keep myself from bursting into tears, my lip quivering with the effort. A few hot tears rolled down my face which Bryan quickly caught with his thumb. "God, I'm such an asshole," he whispered. "After everything that happened tonight…"

Bryan pulled me close to his bare chest again, protectively. The heat from the fire had warmed the air and for the first time since Rick had arrived at the party, I felt safe. My fingers nestled into the thick patch of hair on his chest. "You don't hate me?" I whispered.

He clutched me tighter, a curse escaping his lips. "How could I hate you? Everything you did, you did out of love." He kissed the top of my head fiercely. "That bastard used you, took advantage of you."

How could he say that? Couldn't he see I was doing the same thing to him? I'd gotten so good at manipulating people, I feared I was deceiving him without even being aware. Although they felt real, how could I tell my genuine emotions from the ones I used to get what I wanted? I tried to scream, "Save yourself! Get away from me," but I was too exhausted. Deep down, I knew it was futile. He wouldn't go. The warmth finally seeped into my bones and I felt my head begin to droop.

Bryan gently helped me to my feet, wrapping me tightly in the blanket and led me to the mattress. He kissed me on the forehead and stepped away, my hand shot out to grab him. “Please, stay with me,” I said sleepily.

“Are you sure?”

“Mmmhmm,” I nodded. I was faintly aware of him throwing a few more logs on the fire, the crackling sound like music to my ears. The bed rocked as he crawled in beside me, draping his arm over my waist. Thankfully, I fell into a deep, dreamless sleep.

I woke the next morning completely disoriented, the blissful amnesia of sleep holding on a few moments after I opened my eyes. The events, both good and bad, came crashing down like a ten foot wave. Rolling over in the bed, I looked for Bryan but found myself alone. I shot up, a surge of panic stabbing my chest. The hunting cabin was awash in morning light, the smell of bacon thick on the air. An old cast iron griddle pan was spitting on top of the stove, beside it a kettle that looked like something from a museum.

Flinging the blanket from my body and swinging my feet over the edge, I surged to my feet, half expecting Rick to walk in from the bathroom or something. Just then, Bryan appeared in the front door carrying a heavy canvas tote of wood. His expression lit up when he saw me.

"Merry Christmas Eve," he said cheerfully, shutting the door behind him. He dropped the wood by the fire and shed his jacket.

"God, yeah. It is, isn't it?" It didn't feel right. Rick trying to kidnap me, running away in the middle of the night…these weren't things that happened during Christmas. I pulled my hair into a low ponytail as I watched Bryan busy himself around the kitchen.

"I know it's probably not what you were expecting, but…" He pulled the bacon from the pan and let it dry on a paper towel. "You like fried eggs?"

I nodded, still half asleep. "Yeah, fine." I pulled out a rickety wooden chair and sat at the tiny, round table he'd set. "So what's the plan then?"

"I called Walt just before you woke up, told him what happened. He's got friends around town who'll keep an eye out for Rick and his truck." Bryan set down two plates filled with crispy bacon, two fried eggs, and buttered toast. I looked up in surprise. "What?" he grinned. "I promised you a meal, this is a meal."

"No, it's good. I'm impressed you whipped this together."

A faint blush touched his cheeks as he spun back to the stove. "It's nothing. I grabbed food randomly last night and managed to pack something resembling breakfast. Expect the meals to get much stranger as time wears on." I reached out and touched his hand softly.

"Thank you." I smiled as his blush deepened, somehow making his hazel eyes shine.

It felt both good and bad to be sitting across from

someone who knew pretty much every one of my dark secrets. He knew about Rick and hadn't run. He knew about my mother and could actually relate. It was unnerving. Plus, I felt like it was inevitable I'd find some way to screw it up. However, my confession was incomplete. He still didn't know the real reason Rick was after me. I ate half the breakfast because I was starving, but my worry killed any remaining hunger. My mind was at war with itself. *Can I actually tell him? I have to. He's going to freak out. He hasn't so far, give him credit for that.*

The percolating coffee on the stove grew louder, drawing Bryan's attention away. I cleared my throat and braced myself. *Just one more piece and he knows everything. You can do this little bit more.*

"So…everything I told you last night," I started hesitantly. His shoulder's stilled for a moment, just a second, as I spoke.

"Yeah?"

I tried to swallow the lump in my throat. "It's just…there's something else." I already felt myself choking up. I had never, ever said the words out loud. I wasn't even sure how I could phrase it.

Bryan poured the coffee in two old, mismatched cups.

He set them down and dragged his chair over to me, gently brushing my cheek with his hand. "I don't care about any of that, you know. Honestly, you're one of the bravest people I think I've ever—"

"It's not that," I said quickly, pulling his hands down to my lap. "I need to tell you the last part about Rick." His jaw tightened at the name but he remained silent. I took a deep breath and braced myself, forcing the words out in one big exhalation. "Rick bought my virginity and I promised to sleep with him when I turn twenty-one." My heart thudded in my chest. Somehow, it didn't sound so bad when I said it out loud. It sounded almost ridiculous, like the punchline to a joke. I nearly laughed but the reality of the situation was far darker.

"He…bought your virginity?" Bryan whispered.

I nodded, unable to meet his eyes. I wasn't strong enough to see the judgment there. "He gave me the money up front. A quarter of a million, enough to by my parents old house." I chuckled bitterly. "I guess everyone does have their price. I accepted the deal on one condition, that he wait until my twenty-first birthday. I couldn't believe anyone would pay that kind of money for something so…I don't know…I didn't realize then that he wasn't buying *that*. He was buying *me.* I was dumb enough to think I was playing him, somehow."

Bryan looked out the side window. I lifted my eyes enough to see the muscles in his jaw clenching. *God, he hates me now,* I thought, a fresh wave of tears flowing down my face. "And that's why he's here? Because you're turning twenty-one?"

"I thought if I bought myself some time, I could figure out a way to get around it. When he got arrested, I saw it as my chance to put him away, get rid of him long enough to get away for good."

He squeezed my hands, looking at me intently. "Can't you just give him the money back? You still have it, right?" Inside, I was cautiously optimistic that he didn't hate me. At least he didn't immediately start calling me a whore or something.

I shook my head, my tears falling onto our laced fingers.. "Rick doesn't work that way. He never cared about the money. I could give it back with interest and it wouldn't make a difference."

"You just said everyone has a price."

I cringed at the words thrown back at me. "Yeah, well, whatever his might be, I know I can't afford it. When he comes to collect, he always gets what he's looking for. I didn't know who he was until it was too late." The thought of Rick laying a hand on me made me shudder. At one point in my life, I'd been attracted to him but now…he repulsed me in ways I hadn't thought possible.

"I won't let anything happen to you, I promise," he whispered. "It's all in the past and really," he stopped and looked around the cabin, "there's nothing you can about the past. We only have a choice in the future."

"So you still don't hate me?" I said, peering up through my eyelashes.

He shook his head, but his expression didn't soften. "Of course not. I do have a question, though. The other night at the party, Noah said something about *him* calling Rick. Was Kayla the one who…"

"I don't know, probably. If she did, she didn't mean anything by it," I sighed. "She doesn't know anything about what I just told you. She had no way of knowing…" Bryan nodded, looking back to our hands. It seemed like a perfectly simple explanation but it didn't feel right. My mind tripped over it a few times before pushing it to the side.

"How long do you think we need to stay out here?"

"Well, I wanted to talk to you about that. It'll take half

the day, but I can get you to Denver and on a flight back to North Carolina. You could spend Christmas with your father—"

"No!" I interrupted, the fear pulsing through me like I'd been shocked. "No. I can't do that. I can't bring Rick right to my dad's doorstep. He can't ever find out about what I've done."

"Won't he find out when you give him all that money? You're supposed to be a poor college kid and you're buying houses?"

It was a problem I hadn't yet solved but it didn't let it stop me. "I'll just avoid any direct questions and—"

Bryan started laughing. "He's just going to accept all that money, no questions asked? Come on. I haven't met the guy and I know that's bullshit."

My temper flared. I shoved the plate away with a clatter and stormed across the room. "I don't have much of a fucking choice, okay? If you have a better idea, I'd love to hear it. But for right now, no. I'm not going home." I crossed my arms over my chest and stared out the window, the shrillness of my voice echoing through my ears.

Bryan's chair rattled against the floor as he stood, his footsteps light behind me. He touched my back but didn't push the contact any further. “I’m sorry, that was out of line. Maybe you could buy one of those fake lottery tickets and convince him you won?”

I giggled despite myself. I was starting to feel manic, my emotions running the gamut at the drop of a hat. “That’s actually not a bad idea,” I conceded.

He rubbed my shoulders, his thumbs lightly digging into my aching muscles. It might’ve been a dreamless sleep, but the mattress had left much to be desired. I leaned into him, allowing his arms to circle around me. “Do you have any other family?” he asked softly. I shook my head. After my mom died, her side of the family pretty much disappeared. I reminded them too much of the loss, apparently. Every time my grandmother had looked into my eyes, she’d burst into tears, crying my mother’s name. Bryan’s voice pulled me from the painful memory.

“I’d take you to my mom’s but like you said, I don’t want to bring this guy to their doorstep.” He paused for a moment, holding his breath. “I do have a bit of money…” he added hesitantly. “We could go somewhere completely out there, someplace he’d never think to look?”

“Vegas?” I excitedly responded. I turned in his arms, peering up into his eyes.

He laughed. “What’s in Vegas?”

“I have no idea, but I’ve always wanted to go. Maybe I can win a lucky roulette spin and explain the money that way.”

Bryan’s lips brushed my forehead softly. “Then we’ll go to Vegas. I bet they host a hell of a Christmas.”

“Honestly, I feel safe here,” I said pressing myself against his chest. “If we left, I’d be looking over my shoulder the entire time. He’d follow us. One way or another, he’d find me.” He nodded, kissing the top of my head again. “I don’t know what to do next, but I don’t think having Christmas here is such a bad idea.”

The modest cabin was tucked away in a beautiful, old forest. After we'd cleaned up breakfast, Bryan had suggested we go for a short walk, just to get some fresh air. He helped me put on a pair of old snowshoes and off we went. The snow had finally tapered off to a few flurries. The air was nearly still which made it feel like we were talking around in a snow globe. The truck was covered in a thin dusting, but the snow on the ground was nearly a foot deep.

The quiet forest amazed me, the snow muffling every sound, causing both of us to speak in hushed voices. Bryan pointed out a few deer tracks, but we didn't see anything moving as we walked. He told me about the cabin, how his grandfather had built it with his own hands. I could tell the stories were bittersweet, so I didn't press for anything more than he was willing to give. After a quick loop, always keeping the cabin in sight, we decided to head back. The sun had warmed the water in the tank, so we both took quick showers. Bryan helped me replace my bandages, the wounds thankfully, didn't look like they'd scar. Just as we were finishing a quiet lunch, my phone rang.

I rolled my eyes as I looked at the screen. "It's Kayla."

I wasn't entirely happy with the way she'd handled everything with Rick, but I still didn't want her to worry about me. "Give me a sec," I apologized to Bryan and stepped outside to talk.

"Hey hon, I'm alright."

"Where the hell are you? I stopped by mountain man's house and you weren't there."

I bit back my correction, reminding myself she was upset. "No, we're not in town but we aren't far."

"Tell me where, I'll come get you. I don't like you being out there with some strange guy and on Christmas Eve. We're having a party, remember?"

Her one-track mind never ceased to amaze me. She never seemed to understand how dangerous Rick actually was. Even after last night, she still thought I was overreacting. "I know, I'm sorry I won't be there, but don't worry. I'm totally safe out here."

"Rick stopped by." The sentence hit me like a bullet to the chest. She didn't think to lead with this one? I waited for her to continue, but apparently she just wanted to drop that bombshell and wait for my reaction.

"And what did he say?"

Kayla sighed, the frustration evident in her tone. "He

said what he said last night. He's pissed, Lizzy. You can't blame him for that. He said he wanted to talk but left when I told him you weren't here."

"You didn't tell him where I went, right?" I said nervously.

"How could I? Even I don't know that. Bryan's cabin, that's all I know."

"Good." The word came out breathy, my relief freezing in the air. I toed the snow with my boot, unsure how to end the conversation. Neither of us were going to budge. I didn't want to talk to him, she didn't know when to stop pushing the issue. "So…uh, I hope you have a good Christmas. I'll give you a call tomorrow."

"Are you seriously not going to come back? It's not gonna be the same without you," she whined. I knew what she was trying to do and honestly, the tactic pissed me off. Was she really so selfish she'd be willing to risk my safety? It didn't make sense that Bryan went to such lengths to protect me, a person who didn't know a thing about Rick until a few days ago while she continued to be oblivious.

My voice grew firm. I'd had enough. "Merry Christmas, Kayla," I said and hung up. I stared at the dark phone in my hand a moment longer, shaking my head at her behavior. I loved her like a sister, but sometimes she pissed me off the way only sisters can.

Bryan looked up expectantly from the table as I walked back inside. "Everything okay?"

I rolled my eyes, and shut the door. "She said Rick had stopped by looking for me. She says she didn't tell him anything, but I know she did." I slumped in the sofa.

"Why is she like that?"

"You've got me," I replied throwing my hands in the air. "And then she gave me this guilt trip about how I wasn't going to be there for the party tonight or Christmas tomorrow. We planned this big orphan's Christmas thing. Ugh!" I slammed my fist down on the cushion. Even when I *knew* she was manipulating me, it could work. "Fucking Rick…"

Bryan got to his feet and stood in front of me, holding out a hand. "Are you up for a little fun?"

I looked up with a pout. I wasn't sure I was done with my mini tantrum. "What kind of fun?" I asked with a furrowed brow.

The sparkle in his eye worried me a little. "The kind that gets your heart thumping," he winked. "Consider it my Christmas present. You might want to grab your camera."

Ten minutes later, I stood beside a jet black snowmobile shaking my head. Bryan sat on the padded seat, one helmet in his lap, the other outstretched to me. “No way. No,” I laughed. “There’s no way in hell I’m getting on that thing.”

“Aww, come on! I promise, I’ll take it slow until you feel comfortable. You don’t have to do a thing but sit back and enjoy the ride.” I knew he’d take it easy but the machine looked like it was built for speed. I was wracking my brain for a decent enough excuse when he dropped the only two words that could’ve worked. The dimples forming at the corner of his mouth, he smiled, wiggling the helmet. “Trust me.”

I groaned, taking the helmet from him. “Where’s my Christmas present then?” I whined.

“I’ll give you whatever you want.” His words dripped with innuendo. My heart flip-flopped but I tried to ignore it.

“I’ll be sure to give it some thought then.” I slipped the bulky helmet over my hair, my ponytail pushing down to the nape of my neck. I wanted to look cool, like this whole thing didn’t scare the ever living shit out of me. Swinging my leg over, I tentatively held on his sides.

“You good back there?” His voice was muffled

through the helmet.

I patted him with my right hand. “All good.”

He pressed the ignition and the snowmobile rumbled to life between my legs. I let out a small scream, gripping my arms around his waist for dear life. I thought I could hear him laugh over the roar of the engine. He patted my hand and shouted over the noise. “Hang on tight!”

True to his word, he did keep it slow…at first. He eased us down the driveway and onto the unplowed road, taking the right turn so sharp we skidded a little. Once I got comfortable with the speed, I was able to look up and around. The snow covered pines towered above us, whisking quickly by. The greens and whites were starkly contrasted against the bright blue sky. The ride was so smooth, it felt like we were floating over the ground.

Bryan slowed and patted my hand. “If you’re up to it, we can go off road for a bit. There’s something I want to show you.”

I took a deep breath to steady myself. The road was fine, but a fresh wave of nerves flooded through me at the thought of weaving between the trees. I heard his voice in my head. *Trust me.* “Yeah, let’s do it!” I replied.

A few minutes later, Bryan slowed and cut the engine.

I thought the forest was quiet before but this silence was deafening. I stood on shaky legs and looked all around, the towering pines almost standing guard over us. He pulled his helmet off and set it on the seat. I followed suit.

"There's a waterfall just over there," he said pointing to an outcropping of rocks. "You have your camera?"

I patted my jacket pocket and nodded. "It managed to hang on, too."

The snow wasn't as deep here, the tree branches above holding onto the bulk of it. I followed in Bryan's big footsteps, stopping to look up at the blue sky when I needed to catch my breath. Bryan got ahead of me, maybe twenty feet up the hill. He stopped and smiled, his hazel eyes sparkling in the sunlight. Even after everything I'd just told him, he still looked at me that way. Incredible.

"Do you need me to carry you?" he asked with a cheeky grin.

Hands on my hips, I tried to slow my breathing. Damn cold air showed exactly how out of shape I was. "And what if I do?"

Without a word, he leapt down the hill kicking up powdery snow as he raced towards me. I stepped back a foot in surprise, but his arms were quickly around me. I squealed as he picked me up, clinging to his shoulder. "No, you're crazy! Bryan, your leg!" I wanted to take back the words the moment I said them. His expression wavered slightly as he set me down, the smile now artificial rather than organic. "I'm sorry. I didn't mean—"

Bryan pressed his lips together and shook his head. "Nope, it's okay. You're right." He touched my cheek with his gloved thumb. "You make me do crazy things." His eyes fell to my lips and I yearned for another kiss. God, I wanted him to kiss me again, now that he knew everything. Kind looks were one thing, but I needed to *feel* like everything was still the same.

He seemed to catch himself and the moment dissolved. As he pulled away, I was left panting, but not for a lack of exercise. "It's only up the hill, I promise." He turned and continued back up the slope. I scrambled quickly after.

Once I reached the crest, I couldn't believe my eyes. I'm not even sure I can adequately describe how beautiful the scene before me was. Bryan stood to the side as if presenting it to me, this little treasure of nature. The forest opened just wide enough to allow a deep but narrow creek to pass through. A waterfall, maybe ten feet tall, was lined with glittering icicles the size of my body. Just enough water still ran through the rocks to create the most peaceful burble. I followed the path of the creek down the hill and gasped when I saw the view.

One of the things I still hadn't gotten used to was how limited line of sight was in the mountains. Unless I was standing on the tallest peak, there was always something towering over me. Couldn't be any more different than the flat beaches of North Carolina. But here…this creek cut a swath in the forest wide enough to provide a view to a valley down below. I squinted into the sun to better see the green glade nestled between the soaring mountains, obviously fed by the mountain streams.

For once in my life, I didn't feel like speaking. I simply wanted to exist in this moment, embrace every detail and hold it close. With a start, I remembered the camera in my pocket. As I pulled it out, I glanced to Bryan. He stood with his hands stuffed in his jacket pockets, eyes closed, chin slightly tilted towards the sky. As quietly as I could, I removed the lens cap and knelt in the snow, framing him and the waterfall in the same shot.

I stepped around the creek, snapping photos here and there. I spotted a few deer tracks in the snow on the far bank, and gingerly stepped to the edge of the creek and crouched.

After a few minutes, my fingers were frozen. Putting the camera away, I stood and took it all in again.

"It looks like it's completely untouched, like we're the first people in the world to be here," I murmured in a breathy voice.

"I knew you'd like it," he said coming alongside me. "My dad and granddad used to take me up here." He chuckled, the sound quickly swallowed by the deep snow. He pointed up the hill, beyond the waterfall. "Actually, they used to take me to the lake up there to go fishing but I hated it. I'd always slip away and come down here."

I peered up at him, his cheeks and nose red with the cold. There was always such sadness in his voice when he talked about his family. I desperately wanted to know what'd happened to him but didn't know how to ask. He looked down and smiled, his eyes creasing slightly at the corners.

"I'm glad you brought me here," I whispered. That electric zing passed between us, that undeniable connection we were getting terrible at ignoring.

He pulled off his gloves and dropped them to the ground, sliding his hands into my hair. His lips brushed mine as he pulled me close. He teased the tip of his nose against mine before whispering, "Me too," mouth moving against mine.

I fell into that kiss like it was my first. In many ways, it was. In small pieces, I felt the Liz I'd been falling away to reveal the Liz I wanted to be. The passion and truthfulness we shared in that kiss…it was like I'd never been kissed before. Maybe it lasted a few seconds, maybe a few minutes, but when we pulled apart, I felt like I'd changed in some way I couldn't put my finger on.

Bryan pressed his forehead against mine, our clouds of breath mingling in the air. He kissed me again, full and hard against my lips, before pulling away completely.

"We should probably head back soon. Night comes quickly up here," he said bending to get his gloves. I nodded, taking one last look around the clearing, thankful that I'd been brave enough to come. I had no idea what to expect but opening myself up to the experience had proved worth it.

When we returned to the snowmobile, I gave him a playful slap on the shoulder. "As long as you're careful, I don't mind if you pick up the pace a little bit on the way back."

He gave me a broad grin, one eyebrow arched. "Oh yeah? Ready to get that blood really pumping?"

I laughed, plucking my helmet from the seat and

stepping closer. It was my turn to grab the back of his head and pull him into a hungry kiss. “It already is.” The look of surprise on his face was so delicious. Slipping my helmet on, I nodded towards the snowmobile, Bryan snapping out of his fog.

Wrapping myself tightly against him, this time not out of fear, I was able to enjoy the ride more. He carefully threaded through the trees, following the tracks we’d made coming in. Once we reached the edge of the road, he gave my arm a pat and gunned it. I squealed and laughed, holding him tight. The way he looked at me, the rush, the feel of his hard body beneath my hands, the vibrations of the snowmobile between my legs…it stirred up some pretty wicked ideas.

I decided what I wanted for Christmas.

Bryan

I never, ever, in a million years thought I'd feel this way about someone again. I was overwhelmed when Liz opened up to me. Her mother, her surgery, the things she'd done all for the love of her father. I could see past the actions to the intent and saw nothing but a caring person, doing her best to survive. If anyone knew how trauma could screw with the path of a life, it was me. To say she was amazing doesn't do her justice. I owed it to her to be honest about my past. That was the whole point of taking her up to the falls but I hadn't found the right words, didn't know how to start. Any time I tried to tell her anything about my past, I froze up.

I threw a couple logs in the furnace when we got back to the cabin and told Liz to relax. After I changed out of my wet jeans, I set about making us a modest Christmas Eve dinner. My conflicting emotions became too much to ignore.

I was happy for the distraction of cooking because I didn't think I'd be able to hide my thoughts very well.

Her problems were nothing compared to mine but I still couldn't bring myself to tell her. I felt pathetic in comparison. She'd risen up to the challenges in her life and I'd simply retreated, becoming a shell of the person I once was. I was in too deep, going far too long lying by omission. Would she look at me differently once she knew who I really was, well, who I'd been? Would she hate me for keeping it from her when she'd been nothing but honest?

On top of it all, I wanted her so much I felt guilty. I wanted to feel her bare skin against me, to hold her in my arms, to connect with her in ways I never had before. I glanced at her lounging on the old sofa, one leg slung over the arm as she reclined. She was staring at the ceiling deep in thought. She looked up, giving me that smile I'd almost become addicted to. When I'd decided to move to Tellure Hollow, I thought the solitude was what I needed. Little did I know I'd find exactly what I needed dangling over a bridge, trying to take a photo.

I wiped my hands on the dish towel. "You thinking about what you want for Christmas?"

"Maybe," she winked. Liz kicked her leg off the arm of

the sofa and leaned forward. “I think I’m gonna call my dad. He’ll worry when I don’t come online to chat.”

A dull ache squeezed my heart but I did my best to smile. “Of course. Don’t go outside, I promise I won’t listen.”

She gave a short laugh as she got to her feet, brushing her dark hair over her shoulder. “There’s nothing I could say that you don’t already know,” she said as if the thought had just occurred to her. She sat cross-legged on the bed and thumbed through her phone, giving me a smile as she brought it to her ear.

My mind drifted as I returned to chopping the onions and peppers. The sound of her voice was soothing, just her presence was enough to take away a lot of the burden I carried on a daily basis. As she talked to her dad, laughing and joking, assuring him everything was going just fine, I resolved to tell her everything. I had to at least match her bravery on that. If she hated me, so be it. At least I wouldn’t continue keeping anything from her. Problem was, how to start.

Ten minutes later, the bedsprings squeaked as she stood, pulling me from my thoughts. “Of course I will. You tell Aunt Helen I hope she feels better and give the kids a hug from me, okay?" She nodded as she paced around the room. "Okay, sure. Merry Christmas, Daddy." Her face lit up as our eyes met. "I will. Love you, too. Bye."

"Everything good?" I asked, stirring the veggies around on the frying pan. The garlic chicken in the oven was just about ready.

Liz appeared at my side, her breast pressed against my arm. The contact shot through me like a cannon, my body reacting instantly. She closed her eyes and breathed in deeply. "It smells so good."

"I'm afraid it isn't very Christmasy. I grabbed whatever I could when we left."

"Oh, it's fine. Anything you make will be perfect." With the phone in her hand, she rubbed my arm reassuringly. As she finished speaking, it began to vibrate. She laughed and rolled her eyes. "Dad probably forgot to tell me something. He always does this." She walked away to answer, leaving my side tingling. "Oh! Hey bitch," she answered.

My eyes shot to hers in confusion. Bitch? She laughed and shook her head. "How's it going, *Kayla*?"

Her tone was so different, I couldn't help but listen. She didn't seem to mind, her eyes on me as she spoke, watching me set the table and finish cooking. I could understand pretty much everything just by hearing her side of the conversation.

"Yeah, we're doing okay…wait, what? When was he there? He didn't hurt you right, cause if he—right, yeah. Well he can go fuck himself for all I care…yes, I'm serious. Kayla why would I—no, I'm not going to be at the party tonight…because of *Rick*...I know, I'm sorry. I wish I was there too…yeah, we're still at the cabin. Bryan's actually just finishing up dinner so I—Kayla, seriously. I can't come…please don't…have a good time for me, okay? Merry Christmas…okay, okay…yes, stop! I'm fine! I'll call you tomorrow…alright hon, bye."

Liz sat at the rickety round table with a huff. "That girl, I swear."

I plated the dinner and carried it over, wishing I at least had a bottle of wine to crack open. "Rick stopped by?"

Liz stabbed the chicken breast with her fork, slicing off a thick piece and popping it into her mouth. "He told her he just wants to talk," she said around the food. "It's like she doesn't even care. She's more worried that I'm not going to be around for the party."

"I'm sure she's worried about you," I said, not even

believing the words as I spoke.

Liz chuckled. "Yeah, okay."

As we talked during dinner, I kept trying to guide the conversation around so I could come clean. So many times I lost the nerve. How was I supposed to say it? Just blurt it out? I ran it through my mind, but no matter which way I phrased it, it never sounded right. *Hey, so remember a few years ago when a professional skier crashed qualifying for the Olympics and his dad died on the way to the hospital? You must, it was all over the news. Yeah, that's me.*

Before I could summon the courage, we'd both finished eating and I hadn't said a thing. I cleared the plates and put them in the sink, feeling so dejected. Much to my surprise, I felt two delicate hands circle my waist as I rinsed off the dishes. Liz hugged me from behind, her face pressing against the flat of my back.

"Thank you for making dinner," she whispered against me. "I figured out what I want for Christmas." The tone in her voice triggered excitement deep in my core but I tried to calm myself. Not only was she a virgin, she was a virgin running from a crazy ex. I seriously doubted she'd be in the mood but when I turned and saw the look in her eyes…

"I…uh…" I stammered, my mind turning to mush. I

didn't know what to say as she was gazing up at me through her long eyelashes.

"Come here," she said taking my hand with a smile. As she led me into the middle of the room, I noticed she'd set up a bunch of pillows and blankets on the floor in front of the fire. I'd been so engrossed in my own thoughts, I hadn't even heard her do it! She let go of my hand and sat down in the soft nest, patting the space next to her.

My heart thudding in my chest, I sat down. I couldn't remember the last time I'd been so nervous. Pulling my knees into the crooks of my elbows, I stared into the fire. Liz slid closer, pulling a blanket around both our shoulders. She rested her head on my shoulder, her soft breath tickling the hair on my arm. I had to tell her. I couldn't possibly do anything physical with her until—

"The falls were my happy place," I blurted out. I nearly groaned. Of all the places to start, I had to pick that?

Liz lifted her head and looked at me, but I kept my eyes trained on the flickering flames. "What do you mean?"

"After the accident, when I was going through therapy, I had to picture a happy place. The psychologist told me to pick a place from my life where I'd felt at peace…content, preferably a place I'd visited with my dad."

“I can see why you picked it,” she said softly. Her hand traveled to my right elbow, squeezing it gently as if encouraging me to continue.

I kissed the top of her head. “I was actually a little nervous today. I haven’t been back here since it happened and it’s always been so special to my family. I hoped you’d see what I see when—”

Liz pulled my arm down and nestled into my chest, lifting her chin to kiss me. She gently sucked at my lower lip, pulling a groan from my throat. Her hand tugged at my hair as her tongue swirled inside my mouth. She pulled away, her lips parted and glistening in the light. “Thank you for sharing it with me.” As she pressed into me once more, I held her back firmly.

“Liz, I really think we—”

She smiled sweetly as she pushed my knees down, swinging her own over me like she was climbing onto the snowmobile. Her smile might’ve been sweet, but look she gave me was downright filthy. I leaned back on my hands as her insistent mouth found mine once more. Her lips were mind-numbingly soft and I couldn’t deny the urgency behind the kiss. My right hand traveled to her lower back, pulling her close, almost on instinct. The sound that came from her lips as she ground against my hard cock nearly wiped all my hesitation away. Somewhere, I managed to find my last ounce of self-control.

"Are you sure?" I managed to say between kisses.

Her lower lip jutted out in a mock pout. "Aren't you going to give me what I want for Christmas?"

I cocked my head, running a thumb along that lower lip. "You really want me to be the first?" The idea was exhilarating and terrifying all at once. I'd never slept with a virgin before. Any thoughts of telling her about my past had drained away with the rest of the blood in my brain.

"I'm not sure yet. You gotta round the bases," she said taking my hand from her mouth and guiding it to her waist. "Oh look, you're taking first." She giggled as she pushed my hand up her smooth stomach. I caressed her skin as she wiggled free from her hoodie, revealing a sexy lace bra beneath. Her milky skin glowed in the firelight, her eyes glittering like gems. God, she was beautiful. I leaned forward, sliding up her torso to cup her breasts. I held them in each hand, gently kissing the curve of her cleavage. I gathered her in my arms, pulling her into me, burying my face in the soft skin. Her head arched back, the very tip of her ponytail tickling my arms. Her laugh surprised me. It sounded so carefree. My fingers traced the shadows along her neck and collarbone, before finding the thin black strap at her shoulder. She rocked forward and rested a hand on mine.

"My turn." Her hands gathered the hem of my shirt, pulling it up over my head before I even had a chance to protest. Surprisingly, my first thought wasn't to hide my scars but of wanting to feel her warmth against me. As her fingers touched the red scars on my shoulder, I waited for the questions to come. Sure, she'd seen them the night before, but with her head a little more clear…but as she often did, Liz surprised me. This felt different. She traced the line of my scar down my shoulder with something akin to reverence. For the first time in years, I started to feel comfortable in my own skin.

Liz

I hoped I was putting on a brave face because my stomach felt like a bundle of live wires. I'd wanted to touch those scars from the first night I'd spotted them. There was something about the red lines that drew me in. Maybe it was the way I always treated my own scars…like a sealed window to a deeper, more painful past. As my fingers brushed the raised skin, it was almost like I was touching his accident, feeling the injuries he'd suffered. For a moment, I thought I might be crossing a line.

I glanced up into his eyes, the golden firelight dancing across his features. He smiled reassuringly and a wave of relief washed over me. I hadn't even considered that he might be self-conscious about them like I was. It wasn't just his scars I wanted to touch. His body was incredibly toned, hardly an ounce of fat on him. The muscle was lean and lithe, like a swimmer rather than a weightlifter. My fingers traced a line down his peck to the crease of his stomach, running along the hard edge of his abs.

His hands tickled the sensitive skin on my back as I bent to kiss him again. My ponytail swung forward, dipping across his scarred shoulder. As our lips met, Bryan pulled me close against him, our fire-warmed skin pressing together. I groaned into his mouth as I felt his cock stir under me, a building ache in my core screaming to feel him inside me. Still, I wasn't quite ready to give myself that completely. Not yet.

As the heat built, I steeled myself and leaned back. Taking a deep breath, my eyes locked on his, I reached back and quickly undid the snaps of my bra. In all the times I'd been on stage or in front of another man, I never let them see me completely naked. My heart felt like it was going to fly up my throat but I swallowed and pulled it off in a quick movement.

Bryan's warm hands rose to cup my full breasts, his thumbs idly circling my nipples. The surgery had taken much of my sensitivity, but just seeing his affection, feeling this vulnerable, turned me on. With my heavy breasts, the scars wouldn't be visible unless I laid back, but the scary part was over. I was surprised I wasn't worried about how they'd feel, if he could tell they were fake. With him, it didn't matter. The anxiety in my mind began to loosen and I allowed myself to fully revel in the sensations.

His lips rose to my left nipple, kissing it tenderly before gently sucking it into his mouth. I ran my fingers through his brown hair, head arched back as his tongue flicked across the tip. I instinctively ground my hips against him, the wetness of my pussy dampening my panties. He groaned as I pressed down, the vibrations traveling across my skin. Bryan looked up, his lips wet and open. I had to have another taste.

As we kissed, I took one of his hands and guided it under the waistband of my yoga pants. With our foreheads pressed together, I whispered, "Second base." His callused fingers ran along my trimmed hair, gliding along my damp lips with agonizingly slow speed. Our eyes were locked, seeming to glow in the firelight. Tentatively, he slipped one finger along my wet crease, gliding up and down with increasingly long strokes until he paused on my clit. I moaned as his finger swirled over the sensitive skin. With a sly smile, he slipped back down my pussy, his finger teasing my opening. I ground against his hand, dying to feel him inside.

I kissed a path along his neck, biting into his shoulder

lightly as his finger finally plunged inside. I could tell he was already coated in my arousal. Rocking against his hand, his thumb stroking my clit with soft circles, I found myself nearing the edge so much faster than I'd anticipated. My lack of inhibitions allowed me to really let loose.

Guiding his hand back out, I pushed him gently back against the pillows so he could rest on his elbows. I shimmied down his legs, tugging at the legs of his sweatpants. "I think we might be nearing third," I said with a wink.

He paused, hand gripping his the waist of his pants. "Are we going to—"

I smiled but shook my head. "Not tonight." I crawled back up his torso, my breasts swinging as I moved. I kissed him softly, but nibbled on his lower lip with a bit of attitude. "I do want to taste you though, if that's alright?"

His eyebrows rose in surprise, the corner of his mouth curling as the shock wore off. "As long as I get to taste you, too." My answer was a kiss that traveled down his chest and stomach. My mouth traced the line of another scar, disappearing down below. I tugged at his pants, his hips rising to let me pull them off.

The scar forked near his hipbone, one branch traveling

around the side while the other dove deep into the muscle of his thigh. It was obvious he'd lost a bit of muscle tissue in the accident, a small indent creasing his otherwise toned legs. I took all this in in a matter of seconds, cataloging the blemishes like any other. His scars didn't bother me. I was more concerned with what was nestled between his legs.

I settled on my knees, licking my lips as I took his cock in my hand, stroking him a few times. The silky skin slid over the rigid shaft, a drop of precum appearing at the very tip. Given his relative lean body, the size of it was impressive. I was simultaneously glad and disappointed I wasn't going to try and fit it inside of me that night. My tongue swirled across the tip, his musky scent filling my senses, driving me crazy. I swirled and swirled, broad, flat sweeps that traveled around the head of his cock. I might've been a virgin, but I'd learned how to give good head to compensate.

Teasing him with my lips, I chanced a glance up to see his reaction. He was already moaning, but I wanted to see the pleasure etched across his face. When I paused, he looked down. I held his eyes, my lip curling seductively. I opened my mouth and rested him on my broad, wet tongue while my hand stroked the base. He groaned but kept watching with hooded eyes. Slowly, painfully slow, I wrapped my lips around him and slid down the shaft. My tongue danced along the underside until I couldn't swallow him any further. Hollowing my cheeks, I sucked deeply while pulling back up. Bryan's head rocked back as he groaned even louder, the sound sending a pulse of wetness to my pussy.

"Holy shit, Liz," he moaned.

I don't know how long I teased him. I worked him, I savored every drop of salty precum he gave me until I felt like he was about to explode. I honestly didn't want to stop but when the head of his cock swelled in my mouth, I knew I'd pushed him over the edge. His breath quickened and so did my pace. My lips and hands sliding over his wet cock until he tensed, shooting against the back of my throat. I moaned in response, the sound vibrating through his hardness. Bryan was left gasping, his skin shiny with sweat.

With a smirk, I climbed back up and nestled against his heaving chest, my breasts pressed against him. As I listened to his heartbeat slow, I couldn't help but press my pelvis against him. The taste of him on my tongue, the way he cried my name as he finished…I think he felt my yearning. He turned and kissed the top of my head, whispering, "That was incredible." His hand trailed down my right arm, slipped across my stomach, and delved into my panties.

I was so wet, my pulse throbbing deep in my core with my arousal. He caught my gasp with his lips as he easily slid his middle finger inside. My muscles clenched in response, wanting more, wanting to be filled. He added another finger, grazing the edge of my clit with his thumb. I bucked my hips to every slow thrust, moaning against his mouth. His lips traveled to my ear then down, the steady rhythm of his fingers already driving me crazy.

"I'm gonna steal third," his whispered against my neck. His tongue traced a path down the curve of my breast and whether he knew it or not, just grazing the edge of my scar. He lapped at my belly button, looking up with a wicked smile as he he pulled his fingers from my hot slit. "Help me get these down?"

Without hesitation, I hooked my thumbs into the waistband and tugged off the yoga pants, hot and cool air slipping across my skin. Bryan crawled between my legs, gazing up my body with lust and admiration. He hooked my knees over his shoulders, rocking me into a ball and stealing a kiss before laying back down. Wrapping his arms around my thighs, I could feel his warm breath against my skin. He teased the folds with the tip of his tongue, his fingers working in opposite patterns. The sensation was almost overwhelming, like too many things were happening at once.

He slipped his tongue along my wet skin, sliding it inside, swirling around my tight entrance. I dug my fingers into the pillows at my side and groaned. He stroked my clit with his finger while he plunged his tongue inside, then swapped places with a flat lick upwards. Sucking my clit into his mouth, flicking the delicate skin gently as his fingers delved deep, I arched into him.

Back and forth he swapped these positions, teasing, licking, thrusting. In no time, I was a writhing mess, practically begging for release. The hot and cold air made me feel feverish, like I was going to lose my mind.

I dug my fingers into his hair, pressing into his mouth. “Please,” I whispered. With a low groan, he plunged two fingers inside me as his tongue raced around my clit, my plea met with urgency. Within moments, I exploded with a groan. My pussy tightened around his fingers, pulsing over and over with each wave of pleasure. I cried out his name, pulling his hair, squeezing his head between my thighs. He slowed his pace as I came down, withdrawing, tenderly kissing my swollen skin.

As he slid in beside me, I kissed him deeply, tasting

myself on his mouth. I must've drifted off to sleep because the last thing I remember were his soft lips on my cheek, my neck, his whispers in my ear.

The next morning was like something out of a movie. I was awake first, afraid to stir in Bryan's arms and bother him. I lay on his chest, listening to the slow heartbeat, my head rising and falling with his breath. A slight chill had crept into the cabin as the fire died down, but nothing another few logs couldn't take care of. The floor had been surprisingly comfortable, though I suspected any place where I got to sleep in his arms would be perfect.

The bright morning light soon woke Bryan. I smiled broadly when his first reaction was to pull me close, kissing the top of my head. I burrowed my face into the small patch of hair on his chest, breathing his scent deep.

"Merry Christmas," he whispered, lifting my chin for a kiss.

I gasped. I was so happy just to be with him, I'd completely forgotten what day it was. "Merry Christmas!" I settled on my belly, resting on my elbows so I could look at him. Brushing a piece of hair from his forehead, I sighed. "I wish I had a present to give you."

He smiled softly, reaching for my hand and kissing my palm. "I've got everything I need right here."

There were no words for what I was feeling, the intensity of everything leaving me speechless. We held each other for a few more minutes, watching the faintest snow glitter down outside, slowly waking up.

"Do you want some coffee? I can make it on the stove top and then scrounge something up for breakfast," he said, raking his fingers through my hair.

"That sounds perfect," I cooed, rolling away to let him stand.

I made no effort to hide the fact I was watching him get dressed. When he caught my eye, I laughed and told him he had a hot ass. It was true. I was in awe of his body. The muscle, the damage, the amazing person I'd never expected to meet. He pulled on the clothes I'd taken off him the night before, stoked the fire, and walked barefoot to the kitchen.

Falling back against the pillows, I stretched my hands over my head and yawned. *This is the strangest Christmas I've had so far, but it might just be one of my favorites,* I thought to myself. My right hand fell on my sweatshirt which I pulled under the blankets and slipped into. I did the same for my pants, earning a smirk from Bryan.

"I don't get a show?" he winked.

"It's fucking freezing out there!" I laughed. I climbed to my feet once I was fully dressed and lifted my shirt, flashing him my tits with a cheeky grin. "There, happy?"

He laughed but his expression was mixed. "Like you wouldn't believe," he said solemnly.

Again left speechless, I stood in front of the furnace, letting the increasing heat warm my body. I stared out the windows, watching the slow flutter through the light breeze. I tried to remember the last Christmas I'd spent with my mom. She'd been pretty sick from the chemo and I remembered she'd already shaved her hair off, choosing to wear a fuzzy Santa hat for most of that December. There weren't many presents that year but lots of love. All the girls I went to school with had been obsessed with getting the latest phone or new clothes. I couldn't bring myself to care about any of it, further setting me apart. As I wondered what a psychologist might have to say about that memory, Bryan's voice jarred me.

"Hey, you in there?" he laughed waving a hand in my line of sight.

I blinked, focusing on his eyes. Green this time. "Yeah, just daydreaming." I reached out and accepted the cup of steaming coffee in his hand. "You're a rock star, thank you." I turned, my backside finally warm but my front still freezing. Clutching the cup in both hands, I breathed in the aroma.

"I'm afraid it's gonna be bacon and eggs again. I'll go out and get everything in a minute," he said sitting at the table. He kicked his feet up, leaning back in the wooden chair.

I took a sip of the coffee and heard an engine rev far in the distance, though it sounded strange echoing through the mountains. Our eyes met, both acknowledging the sound. "Maybe they're coming to plow finally?" I shrugged.

"On Christmas morning? Guy must be getting paid triple time for that," he replied shaking his head. We remained quiet as the sound grew louder. It didn't feel right to me but I couldn't put my finger on why. I looked to Bryan who'd swept his feet down, brow furrowed. "I don't hear the scrape of the plow."

That was it. That's what sounded off. A sour panic formed in my throat, the tiny hairs on my neck standing on end. *It's probably just someone driving up here to…to what?*

My mind raced, searching for any explanation than the one I feared most.

Bryan walked to the window, his posture tense but pretending to be casual. The engine was so loud, shattering the quiet morning we'd been enjoying. It was obviously running in a low gear to get through the heavy snow. I gasped with a realization. "What if…the tire tracks lead right up here…" My voice was quiet but panicky.

He glanced at me, pulling his eyes from the window. "It doesn't matter. The truck is visible and smoke is pouring out the chimney. It's pretty obvious someone's up here." He paused, squinting down the hill. "I'm sure it's just a neighbor anyway."

The tone in his voice was far from convincing, but I appreciated the attempt. I clutched my coffee cup for dear life. I'm pretty sure I would've turned into a trembling mess if I hadn't concentrated so hard on keeping that liquid still. The engine revved and revved until it seemed like it was the only sound I'd ever hear. Bryan tensed at the window and I knew the truck was at the foot of the driveway. My heart practically stopped until I saw him relax a bit.

"It's alright. It's not Rick's truck. This one's white. Whoever it is, is carrying on down the road," he said stepping away from the window with obvious relief on his face. Relief was the last thing I was feeling.

"Rick's truck *is* white. He was driving Noah's the other night…" I said my eyes wide. As I finished speaking, we heard the truck stop and slowly reverse. My heart sank. I knew. I knew from the moment I heard that engine it was Rick coming to get me. Walking across the cabin on shaky legs, I glanced out the window to see Rick backing up to the end of the drive and pulling up.

"Fuck," Bryan whispered. He touched my back lightly as he turned from the window. "Alright, get your boots and coat on. We're gonna jump on the snowmobile." I stood frozen. Was this really what my life had become? Running from crazy ex's on a pristine Christmas morning? Wasn't this just a bad dream I could will myself awake from? "Liz!" Bryan shouted. He grabbed my arms and pulled me to my boots. "You have to get ready. I'm not letting him near you, got it?" His eyes burned with anger, his features hardened.

"Okay, okay." I quickly got dressed, my frozen fingers refusing to cooperate. I gave up on tying my laces and just stuffed them inside the top of my boots. It sounded like the truck was slipping up the steep drive, but Rick was coming ever closer. God, what was he going to do once he got here?

A wave of nausea swept through me but I swallowed it down.

"Come on," Bryan shouted as he hung out the back door. I said a silent prayer of thanks that he'd parked it out back. It wouldn't give us much time but every second could count.

I strapped the helmet on as I ran out the door. Bryan leapt on the back, the loud engine coming to life with one try of the ignition. I climbed on, gripping him tightly but feeling very exposed on the back.

"Hang on!" he shouted. I grabbed my wrist until it hurt. I was *not* going to fall off the back of this.

The snowmobile shot forward, heading straight into the thick of the trees. We rounded the corner of the house and I chanced a look back. Rick had parked his pickup just behind Bryan's. He was just stepping onto the ground as we zipped into sight. Everything was a blur, but I could see how pissed off he was. I forced myself to look forward, trying my best not to cry out as Bryan weaved through the trees. He steered us to the road, turning left towards the main road.

Once we hit the open stretch, he pushed the machine faster than ever. I squeezed him with my thighs, hugged him with my arms, and expected Rick to come up behind us any second. The roar of the snowmobile drowned out everything but my fear. Was he ever going to give up?

The helmets made it awkward, but I glanced over my shoulder and screamed. Rick had managed to whip the truck around and was plunging down the driveway at an alarming rate. My heart broke as I watched our little cabin disappear into the forest, a dark curl of smoke coming from the chimney the last reminder of warmth.

I whacked Bryan on the thigh urgently, trying to signal to him that Rick was on our tail. He leaned slightly to get a look in the side mirrors and shook his head. He patted my hands, I held tight, and he went even faster. I could tell he was trying to follow the tire tracks Rick's truck had just left.

I looked back. He was still there but the snowmobile easy outpaced him. Rick was driving like a maniac, though. The bed of the truck was fishtailing left and right. Several times I thought he was going to slide right off into the ditch but he somehow managed to maneuver away. A part of me almost waited for the gunshot to the back…I wouldn't put it past him.

Squeezing my eyes shut, I tried to look a few steps in advance. So we get far enough away from him to what? Get help? Crash some poor family's Christmas morning? Could the snowmobile actually get to town from here? I didn't even know how far away we were from Tellure Hollow. I'd been so out of it the other night, I hadn't paid the least bit of attention to how long it'd taken us to get to the cabin. Maybe we could outrun him and hide? Sneak back to the cabin later and still salvage whatever we could of the day. After that, we'd go to Denver, fly to wherever the hell we wanted and just try…try to…

Hot tears welled up in my eyes, falling down my cheeks before I got a chance to blink them away. In the tight helmet, I had no choice but to suffer through it. I glanced back, fully expecting Rick to be feet away but I saw nothing. We'd just rounded a slight curve, coming into a straight away, so I kept my eyes glued behind us. Nothing. We carried on a few more seconds before I tapped Bryan on the thigh again.

"Look!" I tried to shout. "He's gone."

Bryan glanced in the mirror, slowed, and checked over his shoulder. He drew the snowmobile to an angled stop so we could look down the road.

"He was right there and now he's gone," I yelled.

"There isn't anywhere else he could've turned off." I couldn't see much of his face but his eyes, dark with worry.

Bryan hesitated before cutting the engine, his hand hovering over the ignition. My ears still rattled with the phantom sound, but the silence of the forest quickly returned. Faintly, just off in the distance, I could hear the constantly blaring of a car horn. We both looked at each other knowingly. Rick had crashed.

“There’s nothing we can do…”

“Hopefully he’s dead,” I said with a bitter laugh that surprised the both of us. I shrugged. “Let’s at least check and then we don’t have to keep running, right?”

Bryan nodded once, the snowmobile firing between my legs. I steeled myself for whatever we were going to come up on. As we rounded the corner, I instantly spotted Rick’s truck. It looked like he’d lost control, swerved across the road, hitting one side and then slamming front first into the embankment. The front tires were swallowed up by the deep ditch, leaving the truck tilted at a harsh angle. *At least he won’t be driving after us,* I soothed myself.

As we got closer, Bryan pulled to a stop. I couldn’t see inside the cab of the truck, but the windshield was spider-webbed beyond repair. He left the engine running but climbed off the snowmobile. When I made a move to get up, he waved me down.

“Let me go look.”

I reluctantly nodded but stayed standing beside the idling machine. Bryan approached the truck like he was walking near a wild animal, which, I suppose Rick was. I wanted to scream as the incessant high-pitched horn continued to blare. The passenger side was facing us. He stepped closer, bending to look inside. Closer, closer, until he was at the window. I watched him put a gloved hand up to the glass. He glanced over at me and waved to stay put as he walked around the back. I stepped forward as he disappeared around the other side. My heart thumping in my chest, I started to run towards the truck, fearing the worst when he didn’t reappear immediately. Bryan stepped backwards, looking at the forest around us.

My stomach clenched as he jogged towards me.

“He’s not in there,” he said shaking his head. Bryan grabbed my arm and pulled me roughly back to the snowmobile.

“Then he’s hurt. He couldn’t have gone far,” I said. His behavior was really starting to confuse me.

“We need to go, especially if that’s true.”

I wrenched my arm away, stopping short. “Why? What the fuck is going on?”

Bryan flipped the visor of his helmet up, his dark green eyes urgent. He pulled me close so he wouldn't have to shout. "There were a couple empty boxes of rifle shells. If he's out there, he's close…and armed."

ABOUT THE AUTHOR

For Adele, it all started when she was a young girl sitting on the floor in front of the home bookcase. Searching the family collection, between Koontz and King and discarded Little Golden Books, she found Steel. These alluring paperbacks felt like forbidden fruit. With their colorful, detailed covers, half naked men holding distraught women, how could Adele resist? Oh no, she wouldn't actually read these novels. Adele would just flip through them until the dialogue disappeared and the paragraphs grew thicker. She soon discovered that's where the real action hides. That's where all the heaving bosoms and turgid members were tucked away. Talk about formative reading years!

Adele now lives in bustling, busy New York City with her wonderful husband. She loves traveling, knitting, tequila, coffee, skiing, and her two cats, Penny and George.

Sign up for the Adele Huxley newsletter and get exclusive stories, behind the scenes content, and first dibs on new releases!

www.adelehuxley.com

9383703R00177

Printed in Great Britain
by Amazon.co.uk, Ltd.,
Marston Gate.